"What are you afraid of, Emma?"

She saw concern and caring in Daniel's golden-brown gaze. "The last time I was here, the police found me and sent me back to my foster family." Emma drew a sharp breath. "I can't risk going back to them."

He studied her thoughtfully. Then he nodded, and Emma could feel only relief. She gazed at Daniel and became infused with warmth for this kind and thoughtful man.

It wasn't long before he had pulled up to the house. Emma went to get out. "Wait," he said. He was suddenly beside her, helping her. His hands encircled Emma's waist as he gently lifted her from the carriage and set her down.

"Daniel—"

"*Ja?*"

His intense gaze made her blush. "I appreciate the ride

He nod￼ ntly on her. "I'll ￼ Sleep well, En￼

"Have a ￼ ght, Daniel," she breathed softly. Their gazes locked, and she pulled back, stunned by the riotous feelings inside of her…

Rebecca Kertz was first introduced to the Amish when her husband took a job with an Amish construction crew. She enjoyed watching the Amish foreman's children at play and swapping recipes with his wife. Rebecca resides in Delaware with her husband and dog. She has a strong faith in God and feels blessed to have family nearby. Besides writing, she enjoys reading, doing crafts and visiting Lancaster County.

Books by Rebecca Kertz

Love Inspired

Women of Lancaster County

A Secret Amish Love
Her Amish Christmas Sweetheart
Her Forgiving Amish Heart
Her Amish Christmas Gift
His Suitable Amish Wife
Finding Her Amish Love

Lancaster County Weddings

Noah's Sweetheart
Jedidiah's Bride
A Wife for Jacob
Elijah and the Widow
Loving Isaac

Lancaster Courtships

The Amish Mother

Visit the Author Profile page at Harlequin.com for more titles.

Finding Her Amish Love

Rebecca Kertz

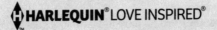

HARLEQUIN® LOVE INSPIRED®

Recycling programs
for this product may
not exist in your area.

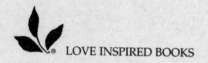

LOVE INSPIRED BOOKS

ISBN-13: 978-1-335-55335-5

Finding Her Amish Love

www.Harlequin.com

Printed in U.S.A.

Ask, and it shall be given you; seek, and ye shall find; knock, and it shall be opened unto you.
—*Matthew* 7:7

For my aunt Betty, my grandmother's sister,
with love. You are a wonder,
and I'm glad I have you in my life.

Chapter One

Crickets chirped and frogs croaked, filling the stillness of the night, as Emma Beiler eyed the Amish farmhouse across the road. It was late, and she realized that everyone inside the house was asleep. She'd come to see the young Amish woman who'd helped her after she'd escaped briefly from her foster home fourteen months ago. She'd have to sleep in the barn until morning, a place she'd sought refuge previously.

Cold, she buttoned up her lightweight navy jacket. She had the feeling she was chilly because she hadn't eaten a decent meal in over a week. Leah, the Amish woman she'd come to see, told her to return if she ever needed her help. Well, she desperately needed assistance now. She had to find a job and a place to live. Maybe Leah could give her guidance.

Emma crossed the street, then entered the barn by the back door. It was pitch-black inside, and once she closed the door, she pulled out a small penlight, the only thing she'd taken with her when she'd left Maryland besides some loose change. She switched on the light and made her way to the stall where she'd slept before. It was empty but laid with fresh straw. The last time, she'd slept with a dog. The puppy had made her feel better as he'd slept beside her when she'd been terrified of discovery.

She stepped into the stall, closed the half door and got comfortable. The scent of the straw soothed her. She was grateful that a horse hadn't taken up residence there. The temperature was dropping, and she shivered. Ignoring her sore feet and legs, she curled onto her side. *Soon, I'll see Leah again.* The knowledge eased her mind, and she allowed herself to relax.

She woke to daylight filtering in through the window over the loft. She'd slept hard and well. She started to rise when she heard the main door open, then the sound of male voices that grew louder as men approached. Emma slunk low into the far corner of the stall and covered herself with straw.

"Do you think 'tis a *gut* idea to build on

to your house, Reuben?" a man said. "Surely it's big enough. You'll have no problem with church service. Missy and Arlin managed to fit everyone inside the house or the barn when they hosted here."

"I don't know, Daniel. Our congregation is growing. I want to do my part."

"You can and you will," the man called Daniel insisted. "Now what did you want me to see?"

Emma froze, terrified, as their voices grew louder. She didn't want them to find her. She wanted to get out without anyone seeing her, then go up to the house to politely knock on the door, not get caught sleeping in a barn stall.

"Back here," the man called Reuben said. "I thought you might want these for your harness shop."

The men's voices were close, and Emma relaxed only slightly as the sound grew distant again.

"Where did you get these?" the man called Daniel asked, sounding awed.

"Picked them up at a mud sale last year. Thought I'd use them, but I find I don't need them. Take them. If nothing else, you can hang them next to the ones you carry once you open up shop."

"*Danki.* If you're sure you don't want them."

"Nay, Ellie has been after me to get rid of them."

"I'll use them," Daniel said. "It won't be long before I have enough money to rent a place."

"Once you open your shop, then what?"

"Then I'll see about finding a wife."

The other man laughed, but she couldn't hear his response. Emma heard the sound of the barn's back door opening and the conversation receding as the men stepped outside. She didn't budge. She hadn't heard the sound of the closing door. Heart thumping hard, she lay as still as she could. After several moments of silence, she thought it might be safe to leave. Relief that she hadn't been caught overwhelmed her, making her feel giddy. Or was the swimming sensation she felt from lack of food? She hadn't eaten since yesterday morning when she'd finished the last of the granola bars she'd bought in a convenience store.

She sat up, then abruptly sneezed as a piece of straw tickled her nose. She stilled, listening for the noise of someone approaching. When all remained quiet, she started to stand, then froze as she sensed someone's presence. She glanced toward the door and saw with mounting horror an Amish man staring at her over the half door of the stall. The man wore a black-banded straw hat, royal blue long-sleeved shirt and navy pants held up by dark suspenders. He had light brown hair and brown eyes. Their gazes locked. The frown on his face eased into amusement as he took in her appearance.

Shame made her hug herself with her arms. She scrambled to her feet, aware of her ragged jeans and the faded green T-shirt under her jacket. When his eyes shifted upward as if seeing something in her hair, Emma instinctively reached up, felt straw and blushed as she pulled it off. When his gaze met hers again, she stared back at him, refusing to be intimidated. She wasn't afraid that he would hurt her. Her only fear was that he'd call the police and she'd be sent back to her foster family, the Turners.

"Did you have a nice sleep?" His deep, pleasant voice rumbled along her spine.

Daniel, she realized, and wondered why it had been easy to recognize his voice. "Yes."

He eyed her narrowly, all signs of his amusement gone. "Who are you and what are you doing here?"

"I came to visit someone who lives here."

The handsome man arched an eyebrow. "Who?"

"Leah," she said. She saw a brief flicker of recognition in his gaze.

"Leah Mast?"

Emma bobbed her head. "She told me I could come back to see her." She bit her lip. "So here I am." She eased across the stall a few steps toward the door, but since he was blocking her escape, there was no place for her to go.

"There is no Leah Mast here."

His tone made her tense. "I don't know her last name, but she has blond hair and blue eyes. A pretty girl."

"You know Leah." He sounded doubtful, but the look in his eyes changed after she'd described her.

"Yes. We met last year." She studied him carefully. He was an attractive man, a fact she couldn't help noticing. "Are you her brother?"

"Nay." He tilted his head. "Come out of there."

Fear washed over her as she shook her head vigorously. He looked nice, but since moving in with the Turners, she'd learned that looks could be deceiving.

He frowned. "You believe I'd cause you harm?"

"No," she breathed, and she believed it, but she couldn't be too careful. "I just need to see Leah. Can you get her for me?"

"Leah no longer lives here," Daniel said.

All her hopes quickly disappeared. Feeling faint, Emma closed her eyes briefly and swayed. Her stomach hurt, and she felt dizzy. "Then I'll go," she said.

He watched her carefully. "I can take you to her, if you like." His smile appeared, but it was gone so fast that she wondered if it had been genuine. "She married and moved into Henry's house. She's Leah Yoder now."

She eyed him with misgiving. Dare she trust him? "Where is she?"

"Not far. Leah and Henry run Yoder's Country Crafts and General Store." Daniel opened the door, and Emma backed into the other corner, hugging herself tighter. Concern entered his expression. "I won't hurt you."

"I know."

"Then stop backing away from me."

She didn't know what to say. Logic told her that he wouldn't hurt her. He was Amish and religious, right? Then she recalled attending church with Bryce Turner and his family, and she knew people pretended to be Christian when they weren't.

Daniel Lapp studied the bedraggled girl in front of him with compassion. The fact that she described his cousin accurately eased some of the concern at finding her in the barn, but not all of it. Leah had lived here with her parents and sisters until each sister had wed and moved away, leaving their parents with a house that was too big for them. After his cousin Ellie married Reuben, the couple had switched houses with his aunt and uncle, her parents, Reuben's smaller house a better fit for the older couple. The trade had worked well since Ellie and Reuben had a son and needed the larger space to expand their family.

Reuben had asked him to come. His cousin's husband had been thinking of adding on to their great room. Daniel thought the expense of a renovation unnecessary, and he hoped that Reuben now agreed with him.

The girl's clothes were torn in several places. He saw a rip near the pocket of her jacket and one across one knee of her jeans. She still had straw in her hair and a dirt smudge across her right cheek. What was her name? How old was she? He scowled at his interest. Did it matter?

"I'm Daniel Lapp," he said, opening the door and stepping inside the stall. "Leah's cousin."

Surprise flickered in the girl's brown eyes, but she didn't move. "You're her cousin?"

Daniel inclined his head. "And you are?"

"Jessica Morgan." She bit her lip. "Jess."

"Well, Jess Morgan, if you come with me, I'll take you to Leah."

She didn't move, and he realized that she

was afraid to trust him. Something shifted inside his chest. *What happened in her young life to make her afraid?* Why was she here in his cousin Ellie's barn? Was she a runaway? Was her family half out of their mind with worry over her?

He softened his expression. "If someone vouches for me, will you let me give you a ride to see her? Leah's sister Ellie lives here now with her husband."

"You don't live here?" she asked warily.

"Nay." Daniel headed toward the back door. "Reuben!" he called. "Would you get Ellie for me?"

Reuben entered from outside. "Why? Is something wrong?"

"There's someone I'd like her to meet." Daniel sent him a silent message with his gaze.

"*Ja*, I'll get her for you." Curiosity glimmered in Reuben's gaze, but he didn't approach. Moments later, Ellie entered the structure, followed by her husband and her sister Charlie.

"What's wrong, Daniel? Reuben said you wanted to see me."

Daniel waved inside the stall. "I'd like you to meet someone and to tell her that I am who I say I am."

Frowning, Ellie approached with Charlie following until the sisters could see inside. Ellie saw the girl in the corner who hugged herself with her arms. His cousin met Daniel's gaze with raised eyebrows. "Who is she?"

"She says she knows Leah. Said they met last year."

Charlie stared at her. "Jessica?"

The girl jerked and looked stunned. "How do you know my name?"

Charlie smiled. "Leah." Her eyes twinkled as she glanced at Daniel before turning back to the girl. "Come outside, Jess. My cousin Daniel is harmless," she said with a casual gesture in his direction. "Most of the time," she added teasingly.

"Who is she?" Ellie asked.

"She's the girl Leah found sleeping in the barn last year." Charlie studied her with compassion. "Are you all right?"

The girl bobbed her head. She started toward the stall door until her gaze fell on Daniel and she halted. Understanding, Daniel stepped back to give her enough space to comfortably leave the stable. "Leah talked about me?" she said, looking upset as she inched toward the door.

Charlie nodded. "She told me not long after she married. She was worried you'd come back and find her gone. She wanted us to know so we could bring you to her if you ever returned. But then you never came back. I told my sister Ellie just in case. She and Reuben live here now." She looked thoughtful. "Leah left a bag for you in the barn for over a week, but you never came for it."

The English girl blushed. "I'm sorry. Something happened and I couldn't come back." She shifted her gaze briefly toward Daniel. "Besides, I'd already taken too much."

Daniel stiffened. Had she stolen from his cousin?

As if sensing his thoughts, Charlie laughed. "She didn't steal anything, Daniel. Leah gave what she wanted her to have." She smiled at her. "Come and be *willkomm*."

His cousins headed toward the door, and he followed. The English girl hesitated as if afraid, until he smiled at her gently and motioned her to join them.

He observed Jess in the bright sunshine and saw a young woman who was vulnerable…and beautiful. Startled by his thoughts, he looked away. When he glanced back, he saw that she avoided his gaze. "Will you let me take you to Leah?" he asked softly.

She didn't say anything but eyed him nervously as he locked gazes with her.

"'Tis fine to go with him, Jess. Daniel is a *gut* man." Charlie eyed her cousin with amusement.

Daniel pretended to glare at his cousin then heard Jess's sharp intake of breath, as if she didn't understand that he'd been kidding with Charlie.

"Would you like some breakfast?" Ellie asked. "I have plenty of muffins and fresh bread. And I can make you eggs and bacon."

"We can get breakfast on the way," Daniel said impulsively, much to his own surprise. He wanted to be the one to feed her. He felt a surge of protectiveness toward Jess unlike he'd ever felt before, and he had no idea why.

"Thanks, but I'm not hungry," Jess said, but he didn't believe her. "I'm fine."

Softening his expression, Daniel captured the girl's gaze. "Are you ready to go?"

"Yes."

"We're pleased to meet you, Jess," Ellie said. She slid a glance toward her husband, who watched curiously. "I'm sorry. I didn't introduce my husband to you. Jess, this is Reuben. Reuben, Jessica, a friend of Leah's."

"Nice to meet you," Reuben said. He handed Daniel the two harnesses he'd given him.

Jess smiled. "Same here."

"Reuben," Daniel said, "Thanks for the harnesses."

Reuben nodded agreeably. "I'll see you

when you get back," he said quietly. "If you don't have time today, don't worry about it."

Daniel watched as Ellie shifted closer to her husband. He could feel the love between the couple and felt a longing for a relationship like theirs. Charlie had the same loving relationship with her husband, Nate Peachy. As did his married brothers, Noah, Jedidiah, Elijah, Jacob and Isaac, with their wives. Soon, he thought, after he'd opened his harness shop.

He set the harnesses in the back of the buggy, then turned to Jess, who now stood quietly beside him. When she would have climbed in, he stopped her. "Nay, over here."

She approached him slowly, cautiously, toward the other side of the buggy where he waited. He glanced at Charlie and saw her compassion for the girl in her eyes. He turned back and held out his hand. "Let me help you," he said.

She hesitated but then let him take her hand. Her fingers felt small within his grip. He reached to place his other hand under her elbow, then heard her gasp and felt her stiffen as he lifted her easily onto the front passenger seat. He climbed in through the other side, grabbed the leathers, waved at the others, then drove out of the yard.

The girl remained silent as he pulled onto

the road toward Yoder's Country Crafts and General Store.

"Are you all right?" he asked softly. She shot him a wary glance, then inclined her head. "We can stop somewhere and eat."

"No." Jess glanced away. "I'm fine," she said, but he sensed that she wasn't.

Daniel wondered again why she'd come. Was she in some kind of trouble? He had so many questions, but he wasn't going to pry. *Yet.*

Less than fifteen minutes later he flipped on his right turn signal and steered the horse into the parking lot next to the store. He felt Jess tense beside him. "Leah and her husband, Henry, own the store. They live in the house on the hill behind it."

She exhaled on a sigh. "I hope she remembers me," she murmured, looking nervous.

Her vulnerability made his heart melt. "She will."

He saw her swallow hard. She seemed to pull into herself, and he felt the strangest urge to offer comfort. He steered his horse up to the hitching post. "Stay put," he said.

Daniel climbed out of his vehicle, tied up his horse, then went to her side and extended a hand to help her. She looked at his fingers, then at him, then placed her small hand trustingly within his grasp. He was gentle as he set her onto the ground before releasing her.

"Are you ready to see Leah?"

Her lips curved slightly. "Yes."

"Come," he said, leading her into the store's interior, which appeared dark after the bright morning sunlight.

Henry and Leah stood behind the counter, going over papers. They both looked up as the bells over the door rang and he approached with Jess. Leah smiled at him before her gaze settled on the girl next to him. She stared a moment as they came closer, and Daniel felt the tension in Jess beside him. Suddenly, his cousin's eyes widened, and she grinned. "Jess!"

The girl beamed at his cousin. Witnessing the pure delight and warmth in her expression took his breath away. In that moment, he realized that she must be older than he'd first thought. A young woman. Something shifted inside him.

"You came back," Leah said.

Daniel saw Jess nod. "I hope it's okay," she said.

"*Ja*, of course. I told you to come see me whenever you…" Her voice trailed off and a look of concern settled on Leah's features.

It seemed to Daniel as if they were silently communicating.

"Come with me," Leah said. She turned to her husband, who eyed Jess warily. "Henry, we'll be up at the *haus*."

Henry nodded. Leah gestured for Jess to round the counter and follow her. As she obeyed, Daniel saw Jess take in Leah's pregnancy and freeze. "I'm sorry. I shouldn't have come. You're about to have a baby."

Leah arched an eyebrow. "And that means I can't talk with you?"

Jess blushed. "Of course not."

"I'll wait for you here," Daniel told the girl.

She opened her mouth as if she would object. She promptly shut it without a word and nodded.

When both women had left, Henry turned to him. "Who is she?"

"Someone apparently Leah knows."

"Where did you find her?"

"In Reuben's barn. It looked as if she'd spent the night there." Daniel's gaze went toward the back of the store where the women had disappeared. He could already envision his cousin making Jess sit and forcing her to eat.

"Should I be worried about Leah being alone with her?"

Daniel hesitated. "I can't say for sure, but my gut says that she'll be fine. She was terrified when I found her. She came looking for

Leah, said they'd met last year. Same way I found her probably. She says Leah discovered her in the barn asleep and offered to help her. I believe she's a runaway."

Henry frowned. "Maybe we should go up to the house."

"We could, or we could trust that your wife is fine and knows what she's doing. Clearly the women were happy to see each other."

Daniel noted Henry's softened expression and affectionate smile. "Leah is something. I still can't believe I'm married to her."

"Believe it, Henry. You're not only wed to her, but she'll be having your *bobbli* soon."

A worried look came to Henry's eyes. "I'm scared."

"Of being a father?" Daniel was surprised.

"Nay, I want those babies more than anything. I worry for Leah and all she'll have to endure to give birth. Reuben's first wife..."

"I know," Daniel said softly. "She died right after giving birth, but Leah isn't Susanna, and she's your wife. She'll be fine."

Henry looked as if he needed to be convinced. "I hope so."

"I know so," Daniel said with a grin. He glanced at the wall clock. He should head to work, but he had to stay to make sure the English girl didn't need a ride. It seemed like an hour had gone by but was probably only ten minutes when he became concerned. "Want me to go up and check on them?"

"And anger Leah? Nay. I'll stay right here. You don't want to be on the wrong side of my wife. I was once, and I vowed to myself never to be there again."

He needed to get to work. If he was ever to earn enough money to quit construction and open a business of his own, he had to show up at the job site.

But Daniel recalled Jess's vulnerable expression and knew he couldn't leave no matter how long it took for the women to return. He was torn between wariness and longing, an odd combination of feelings for a woman he barely knew—and an *Englisher*.

If the two women didn't return after a half hour, he'd go up and risk Leah's ire. He would ensure that both of them were fine. The mental image of Jess's face lingered, and he felt anxious for some unknown reason.

Chapter Two

Feeling guilty for deceiving her Amish friend, Emma followed Leah out of the back of the store and up a small incline to a white house. They entered through the kitchen. The room was spotless, with oak cabinets and a pie on the white kitchen countertop. She glanced at it briefly, then looked away and prayed that her stomach wouldn't rumble from hunger.

"Have a seat." Leah gestured toward a trestle table. It was large, rectangular and made of oak with six chairs. "How do you like your hot tea?"

Emma blushed. "I don't know."

The Amish woman studied her with surprise. "You never had hot tea?"

She shook her head. "I've had iced tea a couple of times." Emma managed a smile. "I liked it sweet."

Leah grinned. "Then you'll want sugar in your hot tea."

She watched silently as her friend filled the teakettle with water and set it on the stove. Emma felt like she should do something to help. She was never allowed to simply sit for a moment and be idle in the Turner household. "Can I help you?"

"Nay, I've got this."

"I'm sorry to barge in on you."

"I'm happy to see you, Jess. 'Tis been a long time." Leah paused. "I was worried about you."

Warmth rushed through Emma, overriding the guilt that had crept in hearing her false name on Leah's lips. "You were?"

The woman nodded. "I knew something was wrong when we met. I wanted to help."

"You did," Emma whispered. "More than you'll ever know."

"Tell me what you've been doing since I last saw you."

"When you found me, I'd run from my foster family." Her throat tightened as Emma thought of her deceased parents. "I lost my parents when they were killed in a car accident." She blinked against the tears that always came whenever she recalled that horrible time. "I was eleven. There was no family to care for me, so I was put into foster care. The Turners

are the second family I've been placed with."
She shuddered and hugged herself. "They're
not nice people, so I've run away from them
again." She paused as Leah placed a cup of
steaming tea before her.

"Be careful," Leah warned. "'Tis very hot."

Emma nodded. She added sugar and stirred
it into her cup. She stared at the swirling liquid for a long time.

"Jess?"

"Yes, sorry." She swallowed hard. "I don't
want to go back, but if they find me, I'll have
no choice." She stopped. "A few days after I
left the safety of your barn, I was picked up
by the police in downtown Lancaster." Embarrassment made her blush. "I was searching for food."

"For food?"

"Yes, near a dumpster," she murmured,
ashamed. But she'd been hungry, and hunger had made her do things that she normally
wouldn't do. "The Turners filed a missing persons report." Emma laughed harshly. "Once I
was returned to them, my situation there got
worse." She didn't want to confess about the
abuse, and Leah didn't need to know what
she'd endured before she'd escaped. Leah's ig-
norance would keep her friend safe from harm
should Bryce Turner find Emma again. She

gingerly took a sip of the hot tea. The warmth felt good in her throat. The taste was delicious, just sweet enough to make the brew go down easily. She felt stronger with that one sip.

"You ran away again," Leah said. "Tell me about them."

She looked up from her tea mug. "If it's okay, I'd rather not." She took another fortifying sip. "All I can tell you is that they don't care about me. They are only interested in the money the state of Maryland pays them for my care." She gestured at her clothes. "I was unhappy there. I had to leave, and I need to find a place to work and live until I turn eighteen, when I'll be free from the foster care system."

Leah frowned. "Jess—"

"Please, Leah," Emma said. "I think it's best if you don't know." Without thought, she rubbed her arms.

Frowning, Leah rose and skirted the table. "What's wrong with your arms?"

Emma blushed and looked away. "Nothing."

"I want to see your arms, Jess. If there is nothing wrong with them, you won't mind if I take a look. There is something you're not telling me." Leah paused. "Please?"

She sighed. "If I show you, will you promise you won't tell anyone?" Emma regarded Leah solemnly. "Not even Henry or Daniel?"

"I promise," Leah said, although she looked extremely uncomfortable.

She stood and took off her jacket. Her long-sleeved T-shirt was thin, and Emma resisted the urge to put her jacket back on. Instead, she hesitated, then pulled up her right sleeve as high as the inside bend of her elbow. Her arm was covered with bruises, but the worst of them remained hidden near her shoulders. When she saw Leah's changing expression, she knew she'd already shown her Amish friend too much.

Leah gasped. "*Ach*, nay, Jess. Who did this to you?"

"It doesn't matter now. I'm not going back."

"Your foster father did this?"

Emma nodded.

"I'm sorry."

"For what?" Emma gazed at her, confused.

"For what was done to you."

She smiled. "You've been very kind, and you've made a difference in my life from the first moment I met you." Emma held her gaze. "You gave me food and the twenty dollars you left for me when I came back the next night."

Leah arched an eyebrow. "What twenty dollars?" But there was warmth in her pretty blue eyes and a smile on her lips. Leah Yoder was genuinely beautiful inside and out.

Emma was relieved to be here with the young Amish woman. She'd never felt so safe since she'd been sent to live with the Turners. It was as if Leah was a true friend, and she definitely needed one. She thought of Daniel Lapp and the way he'd looked at her, as if she'd come to cause trouble for his cousin. But then his expression had changed as he'd watched her a little while later. As if he worried about her, despite his concern for his family. She was wrong. She shouldn't have come back, bringing her problems to Leah. She just hoped for some advice, then she'd leave Leah in peace…and safety.

"How long is it before you turn eighteen?" Leah asked.

"Five weeks."

"And you need a job," the Amish woman said.

Emma nodded. "Yes."

"And a place to live." Leah looked thoughtful. "You also need a place where you can hide until you're free of the foster care system."

Looking away, Emma stood. "Yes. I'm not here to cause you trouble. You can imagine what my foster family is like. But you know the area well, so if you could point me in the right direction, I'll get out of your hair." Dread and sadness filled her as she stood. "I shouldn't have come. You have your family to worry about."

"Please sit down, Jessica."

She blinked and obeyed.

"I have a solution to your problem."

Hope flickered in her heart. "You do?"

"Henry and I need help. I'm going to hire you to work in the store. You can live with my parents, who have a spare room. I only ask that you help them with chores if they need it." She paused. "Is that agreeable to you?"

Emma allowed the tears to fall. "Yes," she whispered. "Very agreeable." She inhaled sharply. "But I shouldn't accept. If my foster father comes here looking for me…"

Leah covered Emma's hands with her own. "I'm not worried about him. Besides, he won't find out you're here among us." She smiled. "You'll be a big help to me. Before long, I won't be able to work for a while." She patted her belly. "I'm having twins."

"Twins!" Emma held her gaze. "You must be so happy about them."

"I'm thrilled. I love Henry, and I already love our babies," Leah said gently.

She grinned. "I'm happy for you, Leah. You deserve everything good life has to offer."

"Danki." Leah rose and went to the refrig-

erator. "Now before we do anything else, I'm feeding you, then you can take a shower."

It sounded wonderful to her. She must have said it aloud because Leah laughed.

Emma hesitated. "May I wash my hands before I eat?"

Leah directed her to a small downstairs bathroom. Emma continued to fight tears as she washed her hands and face. Feeling overwhelmed and emotional, she experienced hope for the first time in a long time. Hope tinged with a feeling of concern for accepting her friend's offer. There was no mirror in the room, but she could imagine how awful she must look after days on the road and having slept in the barn.

Emma managed to gain control of her emotions as she wolfed down the turkey sandwich Leah fixed for her. After she finished, she then ate the piece of an apple pie that Leah pressed on her.

"Come with me," Leah said after Emma was done eating.

She followed Leah out of the kitchen, then upstairs to a bathroom with a shower. She glanced down at her dirty clothes and grimaced at the thought of putting them on again.

Leah turned on the shower and adjusted the

temperature. "Wait here a moment." She returned within minutes with clean clothes.

Emma eyed the royal blue Amish dress, and her throat tightened with emotion. "Leah, I can't take your clothes."

"Of course you can. Until we can get you several garments of your own." To Emma's surprise, Leah took her hand. "Jess, think about it. Hiding in plain sight, you can live among us freely. No one would suspect an Amish girl of being a runaway foster child."

Emma hadn't thought about that. "That does sound like a good plan."

"Gut," Leah said, pronouncing it with an accent. *"Gut,* not good. But don't worry, I'll teach you a few phrases that will make your place here convincing."

"Thank you."

"Danki," Leah instructed.

"Danki," Emma said, and the Amish woman beamed at her.

"When you're done here, come downstairs. I'll be in the kitchen."

"Okay. *Danki.*"

"Ja, danki," Leah corrected with a laugh.

Emma grinned at her before the woman closed the door, leaving her alone to ponder her new temporary life. She cleaned up and changed into the Amish clothes Leah had provided. She knew she wouldn't have trouble fitting in. After all, she'd been raised in an Amish community until she was six years old. She knew how to speak high German, although she couldn't let on. She'd have to allow the others to teach her a few words or they would suspect that she and her parents had left their Amish community for the English world and been shunned by their family and friends for their decision to leave.

"We need to come up with an Amish name for you," Leah said. She looked thoughtful for a moment. "How about Emma? You can be my cousin Emma Stoltzfus from New Wilmington, Pennsylvania."

"Emma?" she breathed, shocked by Leah's choice.

Leah smiled. "*Ja*. What do you think?"

Emma smiled back. "I think it will be easy for me to answer to that name."

"What's taking them so long?" Daniel said. He'd brought a stranger into Leah's life and home. He was worried, although Leah said she knew the girl.

"Knowing my wife," Henry said, "she's feeding Jess over a long conversation."

"You're not concerned?"

His cousin's husband shook his head. "Nay, I

know Leah. She has *gut* instincts. If she trusts the girl, then I do, too."

"Maybe I should go up to the *haus*." Daniel couldn't shake the uneasy feeling that had come since the discovery of the girl in the barn.

"You'll upset not only Jess but Leah as well. Do you want to upset your cousin?" Henry asked with a look of amusement.

Daniel couldn't help a smile. Henry had hurt Daniel's brother Isaac, who had been his best friend, and his cousin Leah had resented him because of it. Even though Henry and Isaac had become close again, Leah hadn't liked or trusted Henry until she'd gotten to know the man's true nature. After forgiving Henry, she'd fallen in love with him. Leah had never been happier as Henry's wife. The fact that she would give birth soon added a new, higher level of happiness to the man on the other side of the counter.

"Are you hoping for a *soohn* or *dochter*?" Daniel asked.

"One of each or two of either," Henry said with a smile. "As long as they are healthy."

He laughed. "That will take time."

Henry shook his head. "Nay. We're having twins."

"Twins!" Daniel grinned. "You're in for it

as a parent. You do know I have twin brothers, *ja*? I remember all the trouble they got into."

"We'll handle them," the other man said with confidence. "You forget who their mother is."

Daniel laughed. "I'm sure you're right. Leah is one determined woman."

"Praise be to *Gott*," Henry breathed. "They're back," he said as if Daniel hadn't heard a door open and shut in the back of the store.

He waited for Leah and Jess to appear.

Leah entered first. "I'd like you to meet someone. Her name is Emma." She looked back. "Emma? Come in and meet my husband, Henry, and my cousin Daniel."

Daniel frowned. What had happened to Jess? Had she left as he'd expected? Then Emma entered the room and he stared. It was Jess but not. The young woman standing before him was clean and wore a blue Amish dress, white cape and apron. Leah had rolled and pinned Jess's hair in the Amish way. On her head, she wore a prayer *kapp*. Her hair was brown with golden streaks.

"Jess?"

"Emma," the girl who now looked like a woman said. "My name is Emma." She glanced at Leah, saw his cousin's nod. "Emma Stoltzfus."

"What?" Daniel looked to his cousin.

"Emma, my cousin from New Wilmington, has consented to be our new employee. She will be staying with my parents and helping them with chores."

Henry locked gazes with his wife, then looked at "Emma." "Welcome, Emma. We can use the help around here. Once you get settled in with my in-laws, we can discuss your work hours."

Leah gazed at her husband approvingly before she captured Daniel's attention with a look that pleaded to trust her. Daniel gave a little nod. "Will you take her to my *eldre*?" she asked him.

"Ja." He turned to "Emma." The girl looked different enough for him to almost believe that she *was* Emma, a totally different person from the one he'd found in the barn. Emma Stoltzfus was a young woman while Jess Morgan had been a bedraggled girl. "Are you ready to go?"

She nodded shyly. *"Ja,"* she replied.

Leah grinned. *"Gut!"*

Emma's lips curved into a smile that stole his breath. *"Danki."*

Daniel chuckled. "I'll bring her back tomorrow morning. What time?"

"You don't have to bring me," Jess, alias Emma, said. "I can walk."

"I'll bring you." Daniel kept his tone gentle. "'Tis too far for you to walk." He turned to Leah. "Will you please reassure Emma that she can trust me?"

Leah appeared as if she were struggling. He saw Emma studying his cousin with concern until Leah laughed. "I wouldn't send you with him if I didn't trust him. He's family." She refocused her gaze on him. "Nine? *Dat* will be able to show her what to do for morning chores."

Daniel nodded. "Nine o'clock, then." He gestured for Emma to precede him, then followed her to his buggy. He hoped his cousin knew what she was doing. Emma looked like an Amish woman, but the fact remained that she was still an Englisher—a homeless Englisher who, up until a short time ago, looked as if she'd been on her own for a long while. He'd be keeping his eye on her. Leah might have good instincts, as Henry had suggested, but Leah was pregnant, and her outlook on life had softened with her impending motherhood.

He couldn't let the strange feelings of protectiveness he started to feel for Emma stop him from observing her closely. Until she proved trustworthy, he'd be watching her like a hawk.

Chapter Three

Emma was silent as Daniel steered his buggy toward his uncle's house. The way she'd worked her way so easily into his cousin's life bothered him. He glanced at her numerous times, but she wouldn't look at him. She kept her gaze toward the side window. The fact that she didn't interact with him only increased his suspicion of her.

"Emma," he said, drawing her attention. "If you hurt Leah, her parents or anyone else within this community, I'll see that you're tossed out of it. Do you understand?" Expression serious, although he thought he'd detected a brief flash of fear, she nodded. "And I'll call the authorities."

She gasped and paled, her face so white that he feared she would faint. He hadn't expected that reaction. Startled, he pulled his buggy off the road and parked, then faced her.

"Emma," he said gently, "what's going on? Why are you afraid?"

"The police can't know where I am."

He stiffened. "Why not?"

"Because I can't go back. I *won't* go back. They'll hurt me, and I'll just run away again."

Daniel instinctively reached out to touch her arm. She flinched and shifted away from him. Something was seriously wrong. He eyed her with compassion. "Go back where, Emma?" he asked, purposely using her new name. "Who will hurt you?"

"My foster family."

He felt chilled. "They hurt you?"

She nodded.

"How?"

"It doesn't matter."

He frowned. Something was fishy.

"I wouldn't be here if I didn't have to be."

"How did they hurt you, Emma?"

She shook her head. "It doesn't matter."

Daniel felt anger, even though he knew it was wrong. How could he not when clearly someone had hurt her? She wouldn't tell him, and that was fine. But someday he'd learn the truth. He couldn't stop his protective instincts from roaring up in full force.

"I won't press you," he said. He could only hope that she wasn't lying.

To his surprise, she smiled, a small, shy smile that lit up her face and made him startlingly aware of how pretty she was. *"Danki."*

"How old are you?" he asked, curious. "Sixteen?"

She shook her head.

He experienced warmth as he studied her. "Seventeen then."

She stared at him with surprise. "How did you know?"

"You're seventeen. You've taken a job at my cousin's store and you'll be living with my aunt and uncle. You obviously have no family, and Leah is clearly protective of you. You don't want the police to find out that you're here. That could mean one of two things. Either you're in trouble with the law or you need a place to stay until you turn eighteen when you'll be free of the foster care system." He held her gaze. "I'm inclined to believe you haven't committed a crime." He turned his attention back to the road before him. "Am I right?"

She blinked rapidly, clearly disturbed by his deduction. *"Ja,* you're not wrong."

He smiled. *"Gut* accent."

"Danki."

His amusement died as she carefully played with the edge of her dress sleeve. "Leah is right. This is the best place for you." Although the secret deception felt wrong. "How about I take you to meet Leah's parents—*eldre*?"

"Are they nice? Leah's *eldre*?"

"*Ja*, you'll like them." And he knew they would accept her into their home without a moment's hesitation. "Missy and Arlin Stoltzfus are fine people. Arlin is my *mam*'s brother."

As he drove on to his aunt and uncle's house, Daniel tried further to engage her in conversation and get her to open up. She might be only seventeen, but he had a feeling that everything she'd been forced to endure had made her seem much older than her years.

"What happened to your family?"

"They died in a car crash when I was eleven," she said.

"Brothers or sisters?"

She shook her head. "I was an only child. I have no other family."

Daniel couldn't imagine being alone with no family. He'd been raised with seven siblings. That Jess—Emma—had suffered such loss as a child was more than a little upsetting to him. "You lived with your foster family all this time?"

"No," she said. "My first foster parents were

wonderful." She grew quiet for a moment, then said, "They couldn't take care of me after my foster father got sick." He saw her blink rapidly as if fighting tears. "I don't know if he is alive or dead," she admitted.

"I'm sorry," he said softly.

Talking about her past was painful. Emma stared out the side window and sensed the long sideward looks that Daniel gave her. She faced him. "What?"

"I'm impressed by your courage," Daniel murmured.

"What courage? I ran away from a bad situation."

"*Ja*, you did, and it was the best thing for you. You didn't know what would happen when you left, yet you went. You were brave."

She looked at him and was amazed to see that he meant what he'd said. She gaped, speechless.

He grinned, then turned onto a dirt driveway that led up to a small white two-story house. "Relax," he told her with a smile. "My aunt and uncle are *gut* people. Remember they're also Leah's parents."

She felt her tension dissipate. If this couple had raised Leah, then they had to be good people. A woman doesn't turn out that kind without having a loving family and home.

Emma stared at the house without moving. Daniel's sudden presence on her side of the buggy startled her. His gentle expression eased her fears. He held out a hand, and she accepted his help. Did he suspect that she was bruised? No, he couldn't possibly know about the bruises. It would be some time before they'd be healed enough to no longer be sensitive, but the dress covered her arms enough to keep them hidden until they disappeared. Daniel startled her when he kept gentle hold of her hand after she got out. He released it to knock on the side door of the house. Within seconds, the woman who appeared saw Daniel, and her eyes lit up as she smiled. "Daniel! Come in."

"I've brought you a houseguest," he said. "Leah sent her."

The woman who must be Leah's mother opened the door wider with a huge inviting smile for her. "Come in."

"Emma," Daniel supplied for her.

Emma hesitated until Daniel's hand on her back urged her forward.

"Tea?" Missy invited.

"I could do with a quick cup," Daniel said. "Emma?"

"Ja, danki."

Missy looked at her strangely before she turned to put the kettle on.

"There is something you need to know," Emma began when the woman took a seat across from her and Daniel, who had chosen to sit by her side. "I'm a runaway. Leah is my friend. She's given me a job at the store and invited me to stay in your spare room." She paused. "And I'm now a cousin from New Wilmington."

Missy studied her intently. "Emma?"

"Ja?" She tensed.

Leah's mother smiled. "Welcome home," she said, and Emma was unable to control the tears that overflowed to trail down her cheeks. Tears of relief and happiness that she'd been given a second chance to feel safe and loved.

Daniel studied his aunt, then observed the young English woman seated next to him. He was startled that she'd been so forthright with his aunt. If anyone would be able to make life better for Emma, it was Missy and Arlin Stoltzfus. He drank his tea, ate two home-made chocolate brownies, then rose. "I need to talk with Reuben briefly before I head to work this afternoon." He met the Englisher's gaze. "Emma," he said, "you'll be *oll recht*?"

She smiled. *"Ja,* I'll be fine."

"*Gut.*"

"I'll see you on Sunday if not before," he told his aunt.

"*Ja*, give your *mudder* my best." Missy smiled. "Please tell her that I might not be able to make it to quilting on Wednesday."

"I'll tell her." Daniel's gaze slid over Emma, and he was glad to see her relaxed with a small smile on her face as she moved to stand next to him. He addressed her. "You, I'll see in the morning. I have to be at work at nine tomorrow, so I'll pick you up at eight thirty." He turned toward his aunt. "Will that give Emma enough time to do morning chores?"

Surprise flickered across his aunt's expression, then came understanding. "More than enough time."

To Daniel's surprise, Emma excused herself to his aunt and followed him outside.

"Daniel," she whispered. He halted and faced her. "*Danki* for everything." Her expression was earnest, open and honest.

He smiled. "I'll see you tomorrow."

To his satisfaction, she simply nodded and went back inside. He left with the image of her bright brown eyes gazing at him with gratitude. He didn't want her gratitude. He wasn't sure what he wanted, but it wasn't for her to feel beholden to him.

He drove back to see Leah first. It wasn't afternoon yet, so he had a little time to talk with his cousin about the young woman in her parents' home. When he pulled in next to the hitching post on the side of the building, he waited a moment, his thoughts whirling with questions that needed answering. He got out, tied up his gelding, then went into the building. Henry was behind the counter.

"Is your wife here?" he asked.

"She went up to the house, but she'll be right back."

"I'll wait. I need to talk with her." He paused. "About Emma."

"Leah's idea," Henry supplied.

Daniel blinked. "What?"

"She picked Emma as Jess's identity while she's here, because 'tis a fine name for an Amish girl."

"What did Leah tell you about her?"

"That she lost her parents when she was eleven."

Daniel nodded. "*Ja*, she told me."

Henry looked surprised. "What else did she say?"

"That she ran from her foster family." Daniel frowned. "She didn't say much, but what she fears most is being sent back to them."

"I'm shocked that she told you about her

past. She had a hard time telling Leah, and she considers Leah her friend."

"I think Emma feels vulnerable." Feeling sheepish, Daniel averted his glance. "I warned her against hurting anyone. Told her I'd call the police if she did."

"*Ach*, nay," Henry breathed.

"*Ja.*" He met the man's gaze again. "She was terrified and explained." Something about her drew him in to help her. He didn't know why. She was an Englisher with different ideals and morals. She could be lying to them, but still he sensed something innocent about her.

Her cousin's husband agreed. "Here's Leah now."

"How do you always know when your wife is near?"

Henry's lip curved, and his eyes glowed with warmth. "Because she is my life."

Daniel stared at him. It was clear that Henry meant every word. "You're most fortunate to have such strong love in your marriage."

"You shouldn't marry for anything but love. I know some members of our community accept arranged marriages, but never settle for that. Love might come in time in an arranged union, but to know it beforehand? To feel it deep in your heart? That is *everything*."

"Daniel!" Leah entered the room with a look

of concern. "Did something happen to Emma? Is anything wrong?"

"Nay, nothing's wrong. Your *mudder* welcomed Emma into her home with open arms."

Leah smiled. "I knew she would. *Mam* is an amazing woman."

"I agree," Henry said.

Daniel smiled. Missy Stoltzfus had been an Englisher who'd accepted the Amish way of life and joined the church to marry his mother's brother, his *onkel* Arlin. If anyone understood the concerns of a young English woman in an Amish community she wasn't born into, Aunt Missy would be the one. "Leah," he said, "I have some questions about Emma."

Sighing, Leah gestured toward the chair they kept next to the counter.

"Sit and put your feet up," he told her. "The chair is for you. I'm happy to stand."

His cousin sat. "What do you want to know?"

"First, I'll tell you what she told me, and you can add from there if you can, *ja*?"

Leah eyed him with surprise. "She talked to you about her past?"

He nodded. "Because I scared her, and I'm sorry for that." Then he explained what happened, watching as his cousin's expression went from horror to understanding to pleasure as he said, "She told me she ran from her foster family. And that she would never go back. I don't know what happened to her, but it must have been something bad."

Leah nodded. "I think it was." His cousin smiled. "She trusts you."

"You think so?"

"*Ja.* I'm surprised that she told you anything. She must feel safe with you."

Daniel swelled up with emotion. "Now tell me what she told you."

Leah frowned. "I can't. I'm sorry, but I promised I'd keep her secrets."

"What kind of secrets?" He stared at her, hoping that she'd give them up.

"I promised. You know I don't like secrets. And while I don't like pretending that Emma is my cousin, I will do it to protect her. She's afraid of her foster father, and I'll do what I can to make sure she is safe until she won't be forced to go back after she's eighteen."

He understood, but he was still bothered by the girl's secrets. What if she wasn't telling the truth? Doubts about her slid in to disturb him as he drove back to see Reuben.

Emma had been so distraught when he threatened a call to the police that he sympathized with Emma once she'd told him why she was afraid. He sighed. He didn't need the complication of her in his community right now. He needed to concentrate on work and his ultimate goal of opening his harness shop. He'd been saving for some time, and he nearly had enough money to look for rental property. Daniel knew that Elijah would give him space in his carriage shop for his business, but he didn't want to take help from his brother. He wanted to be self-sufficient in his business. His brothers had made it on their own. He would, too.

The time spent with Leah after dropping off Emma gave him little left to talk with Reuben before he had to head to the construction site to work. He and the crew he worked with were starting a new job this afternoon. A number of subcontractors were working the site this morning. They would take over at noon.

It was late September. Soon the temperatures would drop, and work would ease up. He wanted to get in as many hours as possible. A few weeks working for the construction company should net him enough to quit.

Emma's vulnerable features swam in his memory. He didn't know what to believe about the Englisher, and until he knew he could trust her for certain, he would have to put his family first before his business…even if it meant his plans would be delayed a little longer.

Daniel scowled. He didn't want to put off his plans, but how could he not? The Yoders and Stoltzfuses were family, and if he learned that Emma was a liar and a thief, he'd do everything he could to protect them. Even if it meant doing something he didn't want to do—like call the police.

Chapter Four

Emma gazed at the kind couple who owned the house she'd be living in for the next five weeks. "I'm a stranger, yet you've taken me in."

Arlin studied her with warmth. "Missy explained the situation. The best place for you is here." He smiled at her. "And we could use the help if you're up to it."

"I'd be happy to help. I don't mind work." Relief hit her hard as she gazed at Leah's parents with gratitude.

"Then 'tis the ideal arrangement," Arlin said.

Missy eyed Jess with a frown. "'Tis chilly in the morning. If you're to help with morning chores, you'll need a jacket and a sweater." She narrowed her gaze as she studied her. "I have a sweater that should fit you. You can wear Charlie's old jacket until I can make you a new one."

Emma opened and closed her mouth. "You're going to *make* me a jacket?"

"*Ja.* It will be getting colder outside in the coming weeks, and I don't want you to get sick." The woman eyed her with affection.

"I have a jacket." She cringed. "It's not in the best shape, but if you have a needle and thread, I could fix it."

"I'd rather make you a new one," the woman said.

Arlin caught and held Emma's gaze when Missy turned to put a kettle of water to heat on the stove. "No sense arguing with her," he said. "She'll do what she wants, and you'll not be stopping her." The twinkle in his eyes showed amusement. "We have grandchildren, but she misses having a daughter in the *haus.* You being here means the world to her," he whispered. "She's going to want to spoil you."

"I heard that, husband," she said sharply, but there was a smile on her lips as she faced him. Her smile remained in place as she turned to Emma. "He's right. I'm happy to have you here."

Overcome with emotion, Emma blinked rapidly. *"Danki."*

"We don't say thank you often. We show our

gratitude in other ways. With a smile or a nod or by doing something special for someone," Arlin told her.

Emma nodded. It had been a long time since she lived among the Amish. It wasn't surprising that she'd forgotten a few things. "I guess I have a lot to learn."

"And you'll do well."

"I—ah—does it bother you that I'm pretending to be a cousin? I know it's wrong, but—"

"'Tis the only way to keep you hidden and safe. We are fine with it," Missy assured her.

"Arlin, where's Jeremiah?"

"I left him in the barn."

Missy frowned. "Why?"

"I didn't want to frighten Emma."

"Jeremiah?" Emma asked. "Your dog?"

"*Ja.* We had him at our other *haus* and brought him with us," Missy said.

"Is he black and white? A little fluffy thing?"

Arlin studied her thoughtfully. "He is. How do you know that?"

She blushed. "I slept in your barn when you lived in the other house. He kept me company during the night. I was afraid something had happened to him."

"Something happened to him, *oll recht.* He's captured the heart of my husband. Arlin, go get him and bring him inside before he chews something he shouldn't."

The man rose stiffly and headed toward the door. "*Ja*, wife."

After he left, Missy laughed. "Don't think he's downtrodden. That man does nothing he doesn't want to do."

Emma felt her lips curve. "I see."

Missy's eyes twinkled. "I'm sure you do. We are going to get along just fine, you and I. Let me show you to your room before Arlin returns and you get reacquainted with Jeremiah."

The bedroom was small but lovely with a beautiful brightly colored homemade Amish quilt on the double bed. There was a nightstand on one side and a tall dresser against the wall next to the doorway. The sun shone through the window, brightening the room. Emma had never stayed in such a nice room. The warm feeling from being in Missy's presence was the best Emma had felt in a long time.

Emma felt hope well up and surround her. God had led her here, and she would thank Him every day for what He'd given her. She smiled as she sat on the bed while Missy looked on. "Perfect."

A loud bark from downstairs had Missy gesturing for Emma to follow her. "Jeremiah is back. Come and say *hallo*."

Emma followed Missy downstairs. The little dog saw her, and as if recognizing her, he sprang forward and placed his paws on her legs. She laughed, scooping him up to cuddle. Aware of being watched, she caught Arlin studying her and suddenly felt self-conscious. "I'm sorry." She bent to put him down.

"Nay," Arlin said. "He likes you. You can hold him whenever you want."

She grinned and straightened with the little dog in her arms. "Do you want me to take him for a walk?"

Arlin nodded. "*Ja*, I'm sure he would like that."

Emma saw the leash hanging from a wall peg in the kitchen. "Does he sleep in the barn?"

The man shook his head. "Nay, we usually keep him in the kitchen. I had him outside with me since earlier when I was working in the barn." He exchanged looks with his wife, who gave a nod. "If you'd like to take him into your room tonight, I'm sure he'll like that."

Emma felt misty. "I'd love that." She smiled her thanks, then grabbed the leash and clipped it onto the dog's collar. "When I get back, can we talk about my chores?"

"*Ja*, we can talk about them," Missy assured her. "Hold on a minute." The woman left, returning in a moment with a sweater. "Put this on. 'Tis too chilly today to be without."

She immediately obeyed, pleased that someone cared enough to worry about her.

The air was nippy, but the day was beautiful. She allowed Jeremiah to run, and she laughed as she followed his rapid pace. She walked toward the back of the property, noting the farm fields and the way the leaves were starting to change on the trees on the property. She made sure Jeremiah was ready to go back inside before she started back. She felt different in her Amish clothing, like she'd stepped back in time to when she was six years old and had visited with her grandparents. When she'd gone to school in Maryland, she'd stuck out like a sore thumb in the awful garments the Turners had insisted she wear. But here? She felt more at home than any other place except Indiana, where she'd lived so many years ago.

She wondered if the Turners were unhappy she left. Or had her foster father realized what she'd seen? She hadn't stayed long enough to see him after witnessing that drug deal and altercation behind the small shopping center in the center of town. Bryce would probably file a missing persons report again. But this time he wouldn't find her. Not living here among the Amish. He would be unhappy with her. Taking her in had ensured he received eight hundred dollars a month from the state of Maryland. He'd look for her for that reason alone. But if he had pegged her for an eyewitness to his and his son's crime? Then she was in danger. If she thought for one moment that he would find her here and hurt anyone who had hidden her, she would leave now. And she would do so if she learned that someone was in the area searching for her. These kind people didn't deserve to be harmed for taking her in. But after what she'd seen, she knew it was a possibility, so she would stay as long as she could and hope that it would be enough time. Right now, the police would be on the Turners' side. But once she was eighteen, they would stay out of it, for she would legally be an adult and no longer be anyone's responsibility. She'd be free to come and go wherever she pleased.

Emma refused to think about Bryce Turner and his son any longer. She was safe among the Amish. She'd live and be happy until the time came for her to go. A sensation of sadness filtered through her joy as she recalled that her life here was only temporary. The Stoltzfuses were doing so much for her. She wouldn't take advantage of them. She'd make herself useful, starting right away.

The sound of buggy wheels caught her attention as she led the dog toward the house. She blinked as Daniel Lapp parked near the house and got out as she reached the grass before the walkway to the side door.

"Daniel," she greeted, suddenly wary. "Is something wrong?"

He approached with a large paper bag. "Nay, I left Ellie's and am heading into work. I saw Leah again earlier and she wanted you to have this."

Curious, she approached, took the bag and looked inside. "Clothes?"

Daniel nodded. "Just until she can get you new ones."

"I don't need new clothes." The garments she'd been given were way better than anything she'd owned at the Turners'.

His expression softened. "Need them or not. You'll be getting new garments if Leah has anything to say about it."

Emma laughed. "That's what Missy said, and it sounds like her daughter is just as determined." Her amusement faded. "You think I'm taking advantage of them. Your family. I wouldn't have come, but I have nowhere else to go."

"I wasn't thinking that at all," he replied quietly. "Everyone needs help on occasion.

We are always willing to help others. It's the Lord's way."

She nodded. "Will you come in?"

"Just for a minute." He followed her and Jeremiah into the house. "I see you have a new friend," he said.

"Jeremiah and I have met before, and I think he remembers me." She opened the door and held it for him. "This little guy kept me company and warm the first time I fell asleep in that barn." She stepped inside and he followed her. "Look who's stopped by."

"Daniel," Arlin greeted with warmth.

His wife smiled. "What brings you back?"

"Your *dochter*'s need to see that Emma has enough garments to last her until spring."

"Leah shouldn't worry about me," Emma replied.

"Just accept it," Missy suggested. "'Tis Leah's nature to be concerned." She addressed Daniel. "Tell her that I'll take care of anything else Emma needs."

Emma's gaze locked with Daniel's, but she couldn't read his expression.

She unclipped Jeremiah's leash, then unbuttoned her sweater and hung both on a wall hook. She would take her sweater upstairs later. After Daniel left, she'd have to ask Missy and Arlin about her chores. She'd always loved feeding the animals at her grandparents' farm. Doing chores for the kind couple was the least she could do to repay them for their generosity.

"Would you like anything?" Missy asked him, ever the welcoming hostess. "Tea? Cookies?"

"*Nay, Endie* Missy. I'll be heading over to the construction site. I have to work today."

"Is Reuben still set on building on to the great room?" Arlin asked.

"Nay, I convinced him an addition isn't necessary. It helped that Ellie wholeheartedly agrees with me. Your son-in-law accepted the truth with *gut* grace."

"How's little Ethan?"

"He's fine. Hard to believe he's standing and taking steps. Ellie is *gut* with him."

"*Ja*, he took to her right away. Ellie is happy to have such a wonderful family."

"Not as happy as Reuben, I imagine," Daniel said with a smile.

He left minutes later after promising to pick up Emma to take her to work. "I'll be by at eight thirty tomorrow morning," he reminded Emma.

"I'll be ready," she promised, and then watched as he drove away. There was something about the man that drew her. What, she didn't know.

* * *

Emma awoke before dawn and went downstairs. She was shocked to see Missy and Arlin already up and seated at the table with Daniel Lapp. He looked nice in a green shirt, black suspenders and navy pants. His hat sat on the chair beside him. His brown gaze slammed into hers, and her eyes widened until she managed to control her surprise.

"You're all up early," she greeted. "Daniel, I thought you were coming by at eight thirty?"

He nodded. "I woke up, got a few chores done and decided to stop by for breakfast with my favorite aunt and uncle." He grinned at Arlin and Missy.

"And we love having him," Missy said with an affectionate smile. "'Tis not the first time he's come to break his fast with us."

"I thought I'd get a head start on my chores before I eat," Emma said. She had her borrowed jacket draped over her arm.

"Why not have something to eat first?" Missy said. "There's plenty of time to feed the animals."

Emma hesitated, then, not wanting to disappoint the woman, she pulled out the chair across from Daniel and sat down. Missy pushed a plate of muffins in her direction, then poured her a cup of coffee. "I can do that, Missy," she said. "You don't have to wait on me."

"I told you she'll want to spoil you, Emma," Arlin murmured with a grin.

She sighed and accepted the coffee before she sweetened it the way she liked it. Watching her, Daniel slid a pitcher of milk closer to her. Emma added a dash of the thick liquid, stirred it in, then took a sip. The coffee tasted wonderful. She closed her eyes and enjoyed another sip before she opened them to find Daniel staring at her. Suddenly feeling flustered, she blushed. "What else would you like me to do this morning besides feed the animals?" she asked as she buttered her muffin.

"Not a thing," Missy assured her.

"Can I help with the wash? I can wash and hang clothes with the best of them."

"We'll do laundry tomorrow."

The room grew quiet as the four of them drank their coffee and ate buttered muffins. Emma couldn't remember tasting anything so good since she'd eaten in her grandmother's kitchen. When she was done, she rose and put her dishes in the sink. She grabbed a flashlight from a kitchen drawer. "I'll feed the animals and come back to do the dishes," she said.

Daniel stood. "I'll go with you."

Emma felt her breath hitch as she locked

gazes with him. *"Oll recht,"* she murmured, easily slipping into the language she'd learned as a young girl. She felt his presence strongly as she left the house and headed toward the barn.

"You learn our words quickly," he said.

She tensed, pausing before she entered the outbuilding. "Why are you *really* here so early?" she asked.

There was barely a hint of light in the sky. But it was enough illumination to see Daniel's face.

He gazed at her a long time. "To enjoy breakfast with my aunt and uncle." He paused. "And to see if I could help you with chores this morning, being your first day here."

She felt herself soften toward him. "That's kind of you."

He didn't say anything. Something odd shifted in his expression before Daniel reached past her to open the door.

Emma entered and switched on the flashlight. She waited as Daniel headed toward the back of the barn. She followed. She knew what to do but was willing to take his direction first.

"We'll let the horses out to graze," he said.

She opened her mouth to object, then shut it as their gazes locked. Was he expecting her to argue? Instead, Emma went to the barn's rear door that opened directly into a fenced pasture. Emma started to pull the door but then Daniel was there tugging it with her. It slid open, and she went back to let the first of three horses out into the paddock.

Daniel followed her and led the other two horses together. Emma sighed. She knew how to do this. She'd learned as a child while helping her grandfather. Of course, Daniel didn't know that. Once the horses were outside. She went over to check the horse water trough and saw that it needed to be refilled. As she turned to head back, Daniel stood waiting for her. "The water trough needs to be refilled."

He nodded at her and waved her to follow him. They found buckets inside the barn and left through the front door. Daniel showed her where there was an outside water pump. He pumped the handle after she set a bucket under the spigot. When pail was full, she moved it out of the way and replaced it with the empty one. When both were filled, Emma grabbed a bucket while Daniel picked up the other. She felt sure he had planned to carry them both, but these were her chores, and she wasn't about to allow him to believe that she didn't have the gumption or the strength to carry them out.

They emptied the buckets into the trough.

After that, Emma looked to Daniel to see what he wanted to do next.

"Chickens?" she asked.

He nodded. This time she didn't wait for him but went inside and filled a pail with chicken feed. "Can I let them out before I feed them?" she asked, knowing that she'd done it when she was a young girl.

A flicker of surprise in Daniel's brown eyes as he nodded gave her a feeling of satisfaction. She opened the fence around the chicken coop and threw down feed in the yard. Emma watched with a smile as the hens and one rooster gobbled it up. When she was ready for them to go back inside, she tossed some grain into the fenced enclosure and watched as they headed back in.

"You've done that before," Daniel said after she'd closed the gate and faced him.

Emma nodded. "When I was little, my grandparents lived on a farm." They most probably still did, but she didn't know for sure whether or not they were even alive. A sharp pang in her heart hit her hard as she remembered how much she'd loved her mother's parents. Had they missed her at all? According to her mother, her *grosseldre* would have pushed thoughts of their shunned relatives from their mind. That leaving the community had made them shunned sinners hurt Emma. She'd had a hard time adjusting to the English life as a young child. Eventually, she'd gotten used to it. But she'd still missed her Amish family and friends.

You can never go back. Her parents had drilled it into her over and over, especially when she'd begged to visit her grandparents. After her parents died, she'd felt more alone than ever before. No mother or father. No aunts or uncles. No grandparents or cousins. No one.

"Emma?" Daniel's concerned voice drew her attention, and she realized that he'd called her name several times before she'd looked at him.

"Ja?"

He eyed her with a gentle expression. "Are you *oll recht*?"

She managed a smile. "I'm fine," she lied. "What next?" she asked, trying to distract him from asking any questions.

"We can let the goats out with the horses, then we should be finished."

"That doesn't seem like enough work for me to do," she murmured.

Daniel regarded her with a smile. "I'm sure Missy will think of something else for you to do eventually. 'Tis your first morning. Enjoy it while you can."

Emma chuckled. "I will."

When they were done, they headed toward the house. Emma was conscious of Daniel beside her. Had he come early just to help her get acquainted with her chores? She realized that she should have asked Arlin the night before how he liked the animals cared for, but she'd taken care of farm animals in the past. She didn't think she'd have any trouble. Still, having Daniel beside her as she worked this morning helped. She hadn't given a thought that Arlin and Missy might do things differently here. Emma knew she wouldn't be quick to assume they did anything the same in the future.

"Do you have some time for another cup of coffee?" Missy asked as Emma, followed by Daniel, entered the kitchen.

Emma glanced at Daniel, saw him nod. "That would be *wunderbor*," he said.

A quick note of the time on the kitchen wall clock showed her that it was only seven. Daniel originally hadn't been due to arrive for another hour and a half yet.

"Sit," Missy ordered when Emma hovered, wanting to help.

She took a seat, and this time Daniel sat next to her.

"Did you get the animals fed?" Arlin asked as he cradled his coffee mug.

"Ja," Emma said. She felt self-conscious. "'Tis still early. Surely there is something else you'd like me to do."

Missy smiled as she set down two mugs of coffee. "Did you make your bed?"

Emma nodded. "Of course." She'd made her bed since she'd been old enough to learn how.

"Then relax. Keep my nephew company. You can help with the laundry tomorrow if you'd like."

After flashing a quick, shy look in Daniel's direction, Emma took a small sip from her coffee. "I can do laundry." She could feel Daniel's gaze on her. She avoided looking at him but couldn't ignore his scent—of soap and outdoors.

"Do you need help getting your corn in?" Daniel asked Arlin after a moment of silence.

"Are you offering?"

"I'd be happy to help. There isn't much. With a little help, we could get it done in a morning."

"I could ask my sons-in-law."

"You've got other nephews, too," Daniel pointed out.

"True. James will be busy at his vet clinic, and Henry will be helping Leah at the store."

"I'll be there to help Leah," Emma pointed out.

Daniel captured her attention. His brown

eyes warmed as he studied her. "That would work." He turned his gaze on Arlin. "Joseph could use the experience. Not that he hasn't had any, but he'll be taking over the farm someday, so the more experience he gets the better."

"I'll ask Reuben," Arlin said. "He'll want to help."

Emma immediately pictured the man who was married to Leah's sister Ellie. The woman and her husband were both blond-haired and had blue eyes. *They will have beautiful children.* She felt a longing for something she most probably would never have. A husband and children. What man would want a runaway foster child with no extended family? She thought longingly again of her mother's Amish family, and her chest hurt. Even after all these years, she still felt the loss.

She sat listening quietly to Arlin and Daniel's discussion. At first tense, Emma soon relaxed and enjoyed sitting at a kitchen table with people who obviously cared about one another. Whenever someone asked her a question or her opinion, she felt included, something she hadn't experienced in years. Feeling accepted. Although her time in Happiness would be short, she knew that once she left she'd never forget everyone's kindness.

She enjoyed hearing the conversation among Daniel and his aunt and uncle. She learned about his siblings, especially his sister Hannah, the youngest and only girl, who had seven older brothers. Daniel expressed concern about the fact that it was time for Hannah to go on *rumspringa*. Apparently, Hannah had always been bold, and he was afraid she'd get into trouble in the English world.

Emma was amazed by Daniel's concern for his family. She wished she had siblings to enjoy. A brother or a sister. Either one would have made her childhood less lonely. Her first foster family had grown children who didn't live at home. The Turners' children, Kent and Melanie, didn't want her as a sibling. In fact, they hadn't wanted her at the house at all.

"I guess we should go." Daniel stood abruptly, drawing her glance.

She was surprised that it was just after eight thirty. Emma was startled that the time had gone so fast. "Are you done with your coffee?" she asked Arlin and Missy.

"Nay," the older bearded man said. "I think I'll sit a while longer with my wife."

Emma smiled as she stood and picked up her and Daniel's mugs. She took the dishes to the sink and washed and dried them. After putting them away in the cabinet, she reached for her sweater, which she'd hung on a wall hook, then met Daniel's gaze. "I'm ready."

"Wait!" Missy said. She got up and pulled two paper bags from the refrigerator. "Lunch for each of you." She handed her and Daniel their lunches. "Fresh roast beef on homemade bread. I put a bag of potato chips in there as well." She smiled. "And an apple. You need to get your nourishment." Her eyes crinkled with warmth. "Have a *gut* day. Emma, enjoy your first day at work."

Emma stared down at the paper lunch bag and was overcome with emotion. *"Danki,"* she whispered. She heard Daniel talking with the Stoltzfuses as she headed outside to regain control of her emotions. Daniel stepped outside moments later. She followed him to his buggy and waited, knowing that he would insist upon helping her get in.

"Are you ready for your first day at work?" Daniel asked after she was seated.

"I'm a bit nervous, but I'll learn quickly. I'll make sure that Leah is never sorry she hired me."

Daniel didn't say anything, but she could tell he was worried.

Emma sighed silently. No doubt worried about Leah and Henry, she thought. He'd been reluctant to trust her from the first. *I'll prove to him that I'm a good worker.*

Fifteen minutes later the store loomed ahead and to the right. Emma was quiet as Daniel pulled in front of the building and waited for her to get out.

"*Danki*, Daniel."

"I'll be back for you at four thirty. Leah said you'll be done working by then."

His sudden cool, detached tone made her want to refuse the ride home. "I can walk home."

"Nay, it will be nearly dark by then. I'll be here when you're ready to leave."

She frowned. If she couldn't walk to work, how could she get to the store without inconveniencing anyone, especially Daniel? Emma thought of the times her grandfather had briefly allowed her to take the reins of his buggy. She'd been fearless and *grossdaddi* had been pleased with her. Could she drive herself?

Daniel was at her side of the buggy before she could move. He helped her out.

"I'll see you at four thirty," he told her again before he climbed back in, then drove away.

"Not if I find another way home first," she muttered as she watched his vehicle disappear from sight. The man confused her. She liked him. How could she not? But yet she knew he saw her as an inconvenience.

She scowled as she headed toward the door in the storefront. Did he come to help with the animals because he hadn't trusted her to handle the job?

Emma briefly closed her eyes as she recalled Daniel's kindness since she had told him about her foster family.

Or had he come because he cared?

Chapter Five

Emma was nervous as she entered Yoder's Country Crafts and General Store. Bells jingled as she walked through the door. She hesitated a moment, then moved toward the counter where Leah and Henry stood, blond heads close, bent over something between them. Henry was dressed in a maroon shirt with black suspenders but no hat, and Emma recalled that Amish men took them off whenever they came inside any building, except perhaps a barn. Although she couldn't see, she suspected Henry's pants were also black. Leah looked lovely in a purple dress with white cape and apron. A white prayer *kapp* rested on her pinned-back blond hair. She and Henry made a striking couple.

"*Gut* morning," Emma greeted.

Leah looked up, smiled. "*Hallo*, Emma."

Emma met her friend's husband's gaze. "*Hallo*, Henry." His expression wasn't as welcoming as it had been yesterday, and she wished she could read his thoughts. "Where would you like me to start? Do you need me to restock the shelves?"

Surprise flickered in Henry's blue eyes. "That sounds like a fine idea."

Emma smiled. "I'll be happy to help with that. If you'll show me where to find what I need…"

Leah frowned. "Emma, I don't want you carrying heavy boxes."

"I'm stronger than I look." She locked gazes with Henry, pleaded silently with her eyes.

She saw his lips curve. "I'll show you what needs to be done." He turned to his wife. "And I'll carry any heavy boxes out for her," he assured Leah.

"*Danki*, husband," she heard Leah whisper. The love in her friend's eyes for Henry was clearly heartfelt.

Emma followed Henry into the back room. He showed her a small room filled with stacks of boxes. "This is our storage room." He held the door open for her to precede him.

Emma stepped inside. "Henry," she said, "I'll work hard for you and Leah." She inhaled sharply. "I promise. Leah has been a friend when I really needed one."

Henry gazed at her silently for a long time. "She cares about you," he murmured.

"I know. And I care about her. Someday I'll be able to repay her—and you—for everything you've done for me."

"There isn't any need," he said. As if the topic made him uncomfortable, Henry became businesslike. "Those boxes hold nonperishable food items. You can start with those. I'll carry them out for you."

Emma nodded. "Okay."

"Ja," he corrected with a little smile.

"Sorry."

Henry arched an eyebrow. "No need to apologize." The man grinned.

He carried out two boxes for her, one at a time. The first box held packages of dried corn mix. When she asked him about them, he explained, "Englishers like to buy it. 'Tis the easy way to make dried corn casserole. Have you ever had it?"

"I've tasted it." She'd done more than that. She'd eaten it many times, even after her family had left their community. They'd loved dried corn casserole. Emma hadn't had it since her parents died.

"Did you like it?"

Emma nodded.

"Leah will have to make it for you," he said with a smile. "She's a *gut* cook."

"Missy is, too. I've never eaten as much as I did last night at dinner with your mother- and father-in-law," she confessed. In fact, she wasn't used to being properly fed.

"All the Stoltzfus sisters are fine cooks," Henry said as he set the second box close to where she needed to unpack it.

Emma smiled. "I've met them—Charlie and Ellie."

"Leah has four sisters."

"Four!" she exclaimed.

"*Ja*. Nell is the oldest. She's married to James Pierce, a veterinarian. He was an Eng- lisher who joined the Amish church because he loved her."

"That's…" *Sweet*, she thought, but didn't say it.

"It has worked out for them."

"So, Nell is the oldest, then who? Leah?"

"*Ja*."

"Leah what?" The woman in question ap- proached with a smile.

"Henry is telling me about your sisters. I thought you only had two, but he said there are five of you."

"*Ja*, Nell is first, then me, then Meg is in

the middle. She's married to Peter Zook. They have a little boy, Timothy."

"Who is next?"

"Ellie, then Charlie."

"I like them," Emma said. "They were kind to me." She bit her lip. "You told them about me."

"I told Charlie." Leah looked slightly uncomfortable. "I know I said I wouldn't tell anyone, but I knew I wouldn't be at the house after I married, and I wanted someone to be there for you when you returned."

Feeling emotional, Emma blinked rapidly. *"Danki."* She bent quickly to pull four boxes of dried corn from the case."

"When you're done with the shelves, find me and I'll show you how to ring up sales," Leah said.

Nodding, Emma went to work, grateful that the couple left her alone to do the job, as if they trusted she wouldn't mess up. She put out stock and rearranged shelves, moving the older product forward while putting the new in the back. It didn't take her long. She picked up one box with the merchandise there was no room for and carried it toward the back of the store.

"Emma, you don't have to do that," Leah said.

Emma hefted the box higher. "'Tis light. Only a few boxes left inside."

Leah looked relieved. "When you're done putting that away, join me behind the counter."

She nodded, put the box back into the storage room, then returned out front to get the other one. The box wasn't as light as the first one since it held canned goods, but it wasn't too heavy that she couldn't manage it. She breezed past the counter into the back where Henry saw her.

"All done?" he asked.

"*Ja.* Leah wants me behind the counter as soon as I put this away." She paused. "I moved the older items up front before I added the new. That's the right way, *ja*?"

Henry regarded her with approval. "'Tis correct."

She beamed at him, feeling ten feet tall, then went to join Leah.

Daniel steered his buggy toward the main office of the construction company where he worked. Today they would be starting a new project. The office meeting was to let the crews know where they would be working in the coming weeks. As he drove into the lot next to the building and parked, he couldn't help but worry how Emma would make out at the Yoders' store. Was it a good idea to trust her? How could they be sure she wouldn't steal from them and then flee? If not for work, he would have hung out at the store for a while, see how Emma was doing. *As if she wouldn't guess what you were doing?*

The room in Rhoades Construction was filled to capacity. The company had grown over the past few years. His brother Jedidiah had started working with them first after Matt Rhoades, his former foreman, had formed his own company. Daniel and his brother Isaac had come to work for Matt next. At one time or another, all of his older brothers had worked for the company, even if for just a few days here and there. Joseph would join them eventually, he figured. His youngest brother would be looking for work to earn some extra cash. He would continue to work on the farm since he was the youngest son who would inherit the property.

Daniel sat in the third row of chairs in the room, waiting for Matt Rhoades and other construction managers to speak. He didn't particularly like working construction, but he reminded himself that it wasn't a bad way to earn money for the business he wanted to open. He needed to work as many hours as he could to raise the money in record time. Except now that Jess Morgan had joined his Amish community, he wondered how he could work as often and as much as he wanted. He had to keep his eye on her. No one else seemed to see the danger in her presence. Leah trusted her, but he didn't. If he kept his eye on her, he'd be able to discover the truth about her.

"We have several jobs in the works," Matt Rhoades told the group of men. "Fred is going to give you your assignments. Fred?"

Fred Barnett stepped front and center. "We have several places we need workers today. I'll call out the job and the names of the men we'd like on the project. Daniel Lapp. You'll be at the new house we'll be building just off Old Philadelphia Pike."

Daniel nodded, waiting as others were called, the crew who would be working alongside him. He was pleased with the location of the job site as it was just a short distance to Yoder's Country Crafts and General Store. He'd be able to stop in and buy a soda—and check up on Emma while he was there.

He climbed into an SUV with the rest of the crew. When they got to the job site, Daniel saw the first order of business was to lay block. Someone had already dug footers and poured in concrete. Cement blocks were on pallets close to what would soon become the foundation of the building.

He went to work with the others. It was tedious work, but it wasn't bad. He worked in the front near the road with an English man, Edward Wyatt.

"Time for lunch," Edward said a short time later.

Daniel looked up with surprise. The morning had gone more quickly than he thought it would. Maybe because they'd been in the office for over an hour before leaving for the job site.

"I'm heading over to the store to get a soda," he told his foreman.

"Want Billy to drive you?"

Daniel shook his head. "Nay, it isn't far. I don't mind walking." He walked quickly. The day was warm with a light breeze to keep it from being hot. He hadn't gone far when he caught sight of the store. He paused near the entrance before he opened the door. He heard the jingle of the cow bells on the door as he stepped inside.

There was a woman at the counter paying for her purchases. She was tall, and Daniel couldn't see who was working the counter because of her size. He approached, expecting to see Emma, when he realized it was Leah who worked there instead.

"We appreciate your business," he heard his

cousin say as the woman grabbed her bags and left. "Have a nice day."

Leah sighed, looking tired. Daniel suffered a flicker of anger. Why was Leah working the counter? Where was Emma? Had she skipped out? Leah glanced in his direction, and she smiled. "Daniel, what brings you here?"

"Leah, I have everything you need from the house," a feminine voice said as Daniel caught sight of Emma entering from the back room. She froze when she saw him. "What are you doing here?"

"Buying a soda."

She narrowed her gaze as if she didn't believe him.

"Emma, will you get Daniel his soda? I'm going in the back to sit for a few minutes."

Daniel saw Emma's features soften. "*Ja.* I'll be happy to. You go and rest. Would you feel better if you lie down up at the house?"

"Nay." Leah smiled. "I'll be fine. I'll just make a cup of tea and take a few moments of quiet time." She grabbed a cup and poured water from the teakettle she must have heated up just minutes earlier.

"Leah, go and sit. I'll bring you your tea." She shot him a look as if daring to object.

He watched with amusement as she helped Leah into the back before she returned to make her tea. Only after she fixed it—as if she knew Leah's preference—and took it back to her did she meet his gaze squarely.

She stared at him hard. "What kind of soda?"

"Cola."

"Brand?"

"Doesn't matter."

She reached into the refrigerated case for a cold can. "Anything else?"

He shook his head. "That's all."

"One dollar."

He handed her a dollar bill. She rang up the sale. "Want a paper bag?"

He shook his head, then popped open the can and took a long drink.

"Did you really come here for a soda or to check up on me?"

He studied her, noting her high color. And how her blue dress made her eyes look a different shade of brown. "Both," he admitted. Then he took his soda and headed toward the door. "I'll be back for you at four thirty," he said. He heard her growl of frustration and smiled as he left.

Chapter Six

Her heart thumped hard as Emma watched Daniel leave the store. He had come to check up on her. The fact that he'd admitted it should have made her angry, but it didn't. How could she be angry when she would have felt the same way if their situations were reversed?

Emma fought back tears and raised her chin, determined to make the best of things. She was only here in Happiness a short time. She went to check on Leah and saw her relaxing in a chair, enjoying her cup of tea. "Leah?" she ventured without getting too close. "Is there anything else I can get for you?"

The woman rose from her chair. "I'm sorry. I've sat here long enough."

"Nay, you stay. It's quiet out front. Enjoy it while you can."

She spent the rest of the afternoon cleaning

the store. She swept the floor, wiped the counters and dusted the shelves. She even cleaned the glass on the cold case. Emma ate a quick lunch at one thirty, then went back to work. Leah had come out front for a while and at Emma's encouragement, the mother-to-be went up to the house to rest in her own bed. Henry entered the store a few minutes later.

"Everything *oll recht*?"

Emma nodded. "Not many customers today."

"I'm sure you can handle anyone who comes in. I'll be in my workshop across from the house if you need me."

"Will you be back before I leave?"

He nodded. "*Ja*, I'll be back.

She learned today that her hours would be nine until three each day. She wondered how much money she'd be able to save working part time, especially after she paid Leah for her garments. She didn't mind the shorter hours. It would give her a chance to help Missy in the house more. Daniel wouldn't be able to accommodate her work hours. She'd have to find another way to get to the store.

Daniel returned at four fifteen. Emma saw him immediately as he entered through the front door. Her pulse raced as he approached. "Are you ready to go?" he asked pleasantly.

"I'll let Henry know that I'm leaving."

As she was headed toward the back door, she encountered Henry. "Daniel is here."

"Have a nice night." He smiled. "You did *gut* work here today."

Emma felt a rush of warmth and satisfaction. *"Danki."*

Henry and Daniel chatted while Emma grabbed her sweater. "I'm ready when you are," she said to Daniel.

He inclined his head. "See you later, Henry." Daniel followed her out of the store. She quickly climbed into his buggy without help and waited for him to settle in next to her. He didn't say a word as he picked up the horse's reins and with a flick of the leathers steered his buggy onto the road.

As the silence between them lengthened, Emma felt a familiar tightening in her chest. She closed her eyes and breathed deeply. When she felt no relief, she sighed and gazed out the side window. Her arms ached, and she rubbed them. Fortunately, she wore long sleeves so no one would see the lingering bruises aggravated by the day's work.

"Are you cold?" Daniel murmured.

"Nay." She settled her hands in her lap and stared out the front buggy window.

"Did you have a nice day?" he asked.

"*Ja*. It was enlightening, especially when you came to buy a soda."

He sighed loudly. "I didn't come to spy on you, Emma. I needed something to drink." He shot her a glance. "Does that make you feel better?"

"Maybe." She bit her lip. "I know you don't trust me."

"I don't *know* you," he said. "I can't help but feel concern for my family.

Emma studied Daniel's profile, noting the strong lines of his face. He was a good-looking man. "Henry was very pleased with my work today."

"*Ja*, he told me."

"Does *that* make you feel any better?"

He shrugged.

"You want to believe the worst of me," she accused.

Daniel pulled onto a packed dirt-and-gravel driveway. He parked his vehicle. "Nay, I'm just cautious."

"What does that mean?" She frowned. "Never mind, I don't want to know."

He jumped down and was on her side of the buggy before she had a chance to get out. His lips twitched with amusement as he extended his hand toward her. Emma eyed his long, masculine fingers as she reached her arms out. He lifted her out of the carriage and set her on her feet. She was conscious of his strength, the warmth of his hand on hers before he let go. The scent of outdoors that permeated him teased her senses.

Missy stood at the door and waved. "Daniel," she called. "Have time for a snack?"

Daniel grinned at her. "Sounds *wunderbor, endie*, but I need to get home. *Dat* is waiting for me to help with one of his projects."

"Don't be a stranger, nephew. Stop in and stay for a while another day." She opened the door as Emma headed toward the house. "Come for breakfast anytime."

"I'll keep that in mind," he said pleasantly. "I'll be by to take you to work tomorrow," Daniel called out to Emma. "Be ready early. I have to be at work by eight thirty."

She stiffened, glanced his way, then nodded before she turned away. As she entered the house, Emma heard the carriage move as Daniel left.

Missy closed the screen door after Emma entered. "Are you up for tea and cookies? Or I have milk if you prefer."

"Sounds delicious." Emma wanted to ask Missy about her thoughts on walking to the store instead of having Daniel drive her, but on her first full day with the kind Amish couple, she wasn't yet comfortable enough to approach the topic. She became aware of how quiet the house was. "Arlin not home?"

"He went over to his sister's," Missy said with amusement in her gaze, "to help Samuel with a project."

The same project that Daniel would be helping with? "Where's Jeremiah?"

The older woman smiled. "He's in your room."

Later on, Missy told Emma over tea and cookies that this Sunday was Visiting Day. "We're hosting. I'll be cooking on Saturday. We don't cook or work on Sundays."

"May I help?" Emma asked, well aware of what Visiting Day meant.

"As if I'd ever turn down help," the woman said warmly. "I took out chicken to fry. Have you ever made fried chicken?"

"Nay," Emma admitted. She had never been allowed to cook in her foster homes, and she'd been too young when she'd lived in their Amish community.

"It takes time, but it's not hard." She pulled a plate of chicken from the refrigerator. The chicken had been cut into pieces ready for frying. "Would you please grab the canister of flour from the pantry?"

Missy showed her how to coat the chicken

with a mixture of egg, flour and cracker crumbs with dry seasonings.

"May I try?" Emma asked, and she followed her instructions.

"That looks fine," the Amish woman praised. "Now we fry it."

Missy had placed a large cast-iron skillet on the stove and filled it with vegetable oil. "These won't take long. About fifteen minutes or so."

"Won't it splatter if we put the cold chicken into hot oil?"

Missy looked at her with approval. "*Ja*, if the oil gets too hot. We won't let it get that way." She struck a match and turned on the gas. The burner flamed to life.

Missy used metal tongs to pick up a piece of chicken and set it into the heating oil. The chicken sizzled but didn't pop. She turned to Emma. "Would you like to try?"

Emma picked up a drumstick and placed it into the skillet.

"Go ahead and put in all of the chicken," Missy encouraged.

"When do you go to church?" Emma asked conversationally as she placed each piece of chicken into the fry pan.

"We attend service every other Sunday. The

Sundays in between are Visiting Days like the one this weekend."

After she'd set the last piece of chicken into the frying pan, she looked to Missy for direction. The woman beamed at her. "*Gut* job. Now we watch carefully and turn the chicken a few times while it cooks to ensure the outside becomes a crispy golden brown."

When the chicken was done, Missy gestured toward the oven. "Go ahead and put the skillet of chicken inside. It will help keep it warm until we're ready to eat."

"Okay." She went to grab the skillet.

"The handle is hot, Emma." She handed her two oven mitts. "Use these."

Emma slipped on the oven mitts and reached for the skillet. She grabbed it using both hands, but the weight of it made her stagger. She breathed deeply as she placed it into the oven, then sighed with relief as she pulled off the oven mitts. She didn't realize that she'd been rubbing her arms until she caught Missy watching her with a frown.

"Emma. Did you hurt your arms today?"

She shook her head. "Nay, I'm fine."

"Let me see."

Emma backed away. "I'm fine."

"Emma." Missy's tone was sharp.

She pulled up a sleeve. She heard the woman's sharp gasp.

"You're bruised. How did it happen? I shouldn't have asked you to pick up that skillet."

Emma smiled. She couldn't help herself. Missy fussed over her like she cared. *Like a mother would fuss over her child.*

"I'll have to talk with Leah."

"Nay, please. I'm fine." She thought what to say and decided on the truth. "This didn't happen at the store."

Missy's gaze grew sharp.

"It happened before I came here," Emma admitted. "Please don't tell anyone. I'm okay. I don't want anyone to feel sorry for me. I can work and pull my own weight. And the bruises don't hurt much anymore."

"I don't like this."

She placed a gentle hand on Missy's shoulder. "*Danki* for caring. I'm truly fine. I need to work. You've all been *gut* to me. Please don't let a few bruises make you see me differently."

Missy's expression softened. "I'll not tell anyone if you take a bath later this evening and soak those bruises. And I may have something that will help. Will you let me help you?"

Emma nodded. "*Ja.*" She thought for a few seconds as she looked around the kitchen.

"Mashed potatoes and peas," she suggested. "You wanted to know what to have with the chicken."

"Sounds *gut*."

Later, after supper, Missy made Emma take a bath. She added Epsom salts into the warm water, then left her to soak. As Emma went to bed that night, she felt much better. It was a while before she relaxed enough to fall asleep.

When the sun rose the next morning, Emma was eager to start the day fresh. Then she remembered that Daniel was coming for her again, and she promised herself that she'd talk with him about another way to get to and from work. He might object, but he wasn't the boss of her, and she'd be fine on her own.

Daniel had found her in the barn, helped her to find Leah and stepped in to assist her whenever she'd needed him. Unbidden came the knowledge that if she didn't continue to accept rides with him, she wouldn't see him every day. She drew a sharp breath. The realization bothered her far more than she'd ever expected.

Chapter Seven

Before dawn, Emma fed the animals, then went into the house to help Missy with laundry. With Missy's help she stripped beds, gathered the dirty laundry and put everything into the machine to wash. An hour later she stood at the clothesline in the backyard and hung up the damp garments and linens to dry in the fresh air.

It was close to seven thirty when she finished with the laundry and went back inside. Daniel had promised to pick her up just after eight. He had to be at work at eight thirty, but fortunately his construction job site wasn't far from the store. Unfortunately for her, she would be almost an hour early for work.

The distance to the store couldn't be that far. She could walk. She wanted to walk. Emma knew that she would have to discuss it with him first, though. But she had to remind herself, he wasn't in charge of her. If he didn't agree, then she'd find a way to approach the topic with Arlin and Missy. They would no doubt find nothing wrong with her walking to work. She had to be careful that the police didn't recognize her and send her back to Maryland. Dressed in Amish garments, she doubted they would see her as anything other than a member of the Amish community. It was a common sight to see Amish walking down the road either alone or with others.

It was a warm September. After her hard work that morning, Emma decided to wash up and change into fresh clothes. She wouldn't need a sweater or jacket today. The weather at the end of September was often changeable, sometimes warm, sometimes cool. Today promised to be a warm one. When she came back downstairs, she heard Daniel's voice from the direction of the kitchen. He was seated at the kitchen table, a cup of coffee before him.

"Emma," Missy said with a smile, "Daniel's here."

"Daniel," she greeted. There would be no ignoring the man. She glanced quickly at the wall clock and felt slightly annoyed that it was only seven forty-five with Daniel already there. She started to bring up the subject of walking to work, then thought better of it. She'd talk with Daniel about it later.

"Did you want coffee?" Missy asked.

"Nay, but I appreciate the offer," Emma said. She locked eyes with Daniel. "I'll be outside when you're ready." Her heart pumped hard as she exited the house and went out in the backyard where they'd tied up Jeremiah earlier. She unclipped his tie-out line, then put on his leash. Then she walked him around the yard a bit before Arlin appeared at the door to the barn. "Would you like him inside?" she asked.

Arlin shook his head. "I'll take him into the barn with me."

Emma had recently learned that Arlin liked to make birdhouses, small tables and shelves as well as other wooden items. She'd seen the items in one back corner of the barn set aside for his workshop, and she'd been impressed not only by the craftsmanship but the way he'd painted some of them to sell in local gift shops for tourists. She smiled as she handed Arlin his dog's leash.

"I see Daniel is here. You ready for work?"

Emma nodded. "I know it was only my first day, but I enjoyed yesterday."

"Gut," the man said with gruff affection. Emma heard a screen door open as Arlin

looked past her before he met her gaze again. "Daniel," he murmured.

She turned to watch with skittering nerves as Daniel approached. *"Onkel,"* he said with a smile. To Emma's surprise, the younger man bent down to pet Jeremiah, spending a few moments lavishing attention on his uncle's dog. Both surprised her. Not all Amish cared for animals that didn't serve a specific purpose like a horse pulling a carriage or chickens laying eggs or cows providing milk. Emma had always loved all animals, but this little black-and-white furry creature held a special place in her heart. The dog had been kept in the barn and had offered Emma the comfort she'd desperately needed as she'd tried to get a good night's sleep in a stranger's building. Only they were not strangers anymore. Now she knew that the house and the barn had belonged to Arlin and Missy Stoltzfus.

Daniel rose to his feet. "Ready?" he asked Emma as he placed his straw hat onto his head. He looked handsome in a light green shirt with denim pants and black suspenders. He wore heavy-duty tan work boots. Everything about him proclaimed him a strong male personality. Emma thought of her father, who'd been more studious and quieter, but she and her mother had loved him dearly.

Missy came out of the house. "Don't forget your lunches," the woman said as she approached. She handed Emma and Daniel each a paper bag. "Chicken salad sandwiches," she told him.

Daniel grinned. "My favorite." The sight of his sparkling eyes and smile hit Emma like a brick to her midsection.

"Mine, too," she murmured truthfully.

"We should go," Daniel said. Near the passenger side of the buggy, he held out his hand to her. She drew a calming breath and accepted his help, aware of his warm fingers around hers.

"Did you sleep well?"

She got situated in the front seat of the buggy, then stared at him. "Why do you ask?"

He sighed. "You look tired."

"I'm fine," she said shortly.

Daniel remained silent as he skirted the buggy and climbed into the other side. "'Tis going to be like this, is it?" he said stiffly.

"Like what?"

"You don't like me, I get it, but can't we be… kind to each other?"

She blinked rapidly, suddenly on the verge of tears. Her intention wasn't to be unkind. She'd suffered enough unkindness in her life and hated the idea that she made someone feel that way. "I'm sorry."

He looked surprised as he met her gaze. "I understand. I'm sorry, too. I wasn't exactly kind to you. It was rude of me to suggest that I have doubts about you."

Emma suddenly felt vulnerable and didn't know what to say. "We can start over," she suggested softly after Daniel had climbed onto the driver's side.

His lips curved as he regarded her with warmth. "We could."

Emma decided to wait until the ride home to discuss another way for her to get to work. She wanted to prolong the easy moment between them. Once she told him what she wanted, Daniel would be unhappy with her once more.

The drive to the Yoders' store took less than fifteen minutes. Emma took notice of the speed of the buggy. Fifteen minutes in a carriage that went how fast? Not fast at all, she realized. Therefore, the store was how far? Two miles? She could walk two miles easily enough.

Daniel pulled in front of the store and waited for her to get out. She'd seen his instinctive move to get out to help her, but he'd held back, probably because of her reaction earlier.

She hesitated a moment, then regarded him softly. "Thank you, Daniel," she said sincerely. Without waiting for his response, she headed toward the store. The front door was locked, so she went around to the back entrance, which was open. Upon entering, she immediately saw Henry at the table, drinking a cup of coffee.

"*Gut* mornin', Henry."

He looked surprised to see her. "You're early."

"Daniel had to be at work by eight thirty this morning, so he dropped me off early."

The man nodded. He held up his mug. "Would you like coffee?"

"*Ja.*" He started to rise. "I can get it," she said. She grabbed a mug and went out front to the pot resting on the small single gas propane burner. She poured coffee into her cup, then added one sugar before going into the back room again. "How's Leah feeling?" she asked.

Henry smiled warmly. "My wife is fine. Slept in this morning, and I didn't have the heart to wake her."

"She needs her sleep," Emma murmured with a smile.

He nodded as he gestured to a second chair at the table. "Have a seat."

She stiffened. Had she done something wrong the previous day?

"You're not in trouble. You did a *gut* job yesterday."

She gaped at him. "*Danki.*" She frowned. "Then what?"

"I need to take Leah to the doctor today."

"Is she *oll recht*?"

Henry inclined his head. "*Ja*, just a routine visit."

She felt an overwhelming sense of relief. "What do you need from me?"

"Can you handle the store by yourself?"

"*Ja*, of course—"

"*Gut.*" Henry smiled. "We'll be gone for most of the morning. I want to take her out to lunch afterward."

Emma grinned. "She'll like that. She works too hard."

The good humor left his expression. "She does, but she doesn't think so."

"Give her a day to remember. It will be *gut* for her."

"I will."

Henry left through the back door, and Emma checked that everything was ready for her to open the store. She felt confident as she unlocked the door.

Her morning was uneventful. No customers came by until it was close to ten. Then Missy and Arlin Stoltzfus came into the store together. Emma eyed them warily as they approached the counter. Had they come to check up on her, much as Daniel had done the day before? Still, she greeted them warmly.

"We wanted to see you at work," Missy said

with a smile. The woman looked genuinely happy to see her. "And frankly I need a few things."

Emma nodded. "Can I help you find something?"

"Nay, I know my way around."

She chuckled. "I'm sure you do."

Arlin stood at Missy's side, watching his wife fondly as she pulled a list from beneath the waistband of her apron. "Is Leah up at the *haus*?" he asked.

"Henry took her for her doctor's appointment this morning." Emma met his gaze. "Then he's taking her out to lunch."

The man's eyes warmed. "He's a *gut* man."

"Coffee?" When Arlin nodded, Emma fixed him a cup of coffee and set it on the counter close to him.

A few minutes later, she rang up Missy's purchases and watched as they headed out. "We'll see you at home later," the woman said.

Home, Emma thought as she watched the couple leave. Arlin and Missy considered their house her home.

Wasn't that wonderful?

Daniel was silent when he came to pick her up after work at three. Emma wondered if he'd had a bad afternoon or if it was just her that bothered him. Then she recalled that Henry had set three o'clock as the end of her workday. That would greatly infringe on his own work hours. Another reason to insist on her finding another way to and from work.

"Where are we going?" she asked with concern when he'd gone in a direction opposite from the Arlin Stoltzfus residence.

"Into town. I need to pick up a few items at the supermarket. Things that Leah and Henry don't carry."

"Downtown Lancaster?" she asked, growing anxious. What if Bryce had filed a missing persons report and the police were searching for her? Worse yet, what if Bryce, having recalled where she'd been found the last time, decided to come looking for her himself?

Her heart began to race in fear. She clutched the side of the buggy, her chest tightening as she struggled to breathe. "I need to get home," she said. "Please take me home." Emma swallowed hard. "I have chores to do."

Daniel must have recognized her fear, for minutes later he had steered the horse into the parking lot of a shopping center and turned the vehicle around. He didn't say another word as he drove her home.

Fifteen minutes later, Daniel drove his vehicle onto the Stoltzfuses' dirt driveway. He didn't say anything at first. Emma wanted to get out. In fact, she went to move, but his hand on her arm stopped her. "What are you afraid of?" he asked softly.

She closed her eyes, seeking God's guidance. When she opened them, she saw concern and caring in Daniel's golden-brown gaze. "The last time I was in downtown Lancaster," she said, "the police found me and sent me back to my foster family." She drew a sharp breath. "I can't risk it happening again."

He studied her thoughtfully. Then he nodded, and Emma could feel only relief. She turned to get out.

"Wait," he said. Suddenly he was beside her, waiting to help her get out of the vehicle.

His hands encircled her waist as he gently lifted her from the carriage and set her down.

"Daniel—"

"Ja?"

His intense gaze made her blush. "I appreciate the ride home."

He nodded, his eyes still focused intently on her. "I'll be by for you in the morning. Sleep well, Emma."

She remembered she'd wanted to talk about her walking to work. "Daniel—"

He shook his head. "We'll talk tomorrow. *Mam* needs groceries."

Emma felt guilty for keeping him from the grocery store.

"Have a nice night, Daniel," she breathed softly before she headed inside.

She looked out the window once she was inside and saw that Daniel hadn't driven away yet. He stared at the house with an odd expression. Their gazes locked, and she pulled back from the glass, stunned by the riotous feelings inside her.

"Emma?" Missy called from the gathering room. "That you?"

"*Ja*, 'tis me," she said before she made her way to where Missy sat, sewing, in the great room.

"Did you have a *gut* day?" the older woman asked.

"*Ja*, I did." Emma realized that she meant it, although the drive home had been fraught with tension and worry. Was Daniel still outside in the buggy? Or had he finally left? She ignored the urge to check as she joined Missy by taking a chair next to hers. "What are you doing?"

"Making squares for our quilting bee next Wednesday at my sister-in-law Katie's *haus*." She smiled. "You'll meet her on Sunday. Katie is Daniel's *mudder*."

Would she see Daniel on Sunday as well?

"Tomorrow is your last workday at the store for the week. On Saturday, if you'd like," Missy said, "you can help me with the baking for Visiting Day."

"I'd love to help you."

Missy smiled. "I'll show you how to make an upside-down chocolate cake and a couple of pies."

"I'll look forward to it," Emma said. And she realized that she wanted to learning everything Missy was willing to teach her. She loved that everyone in this community was so warm and friendly. She hadn't felt this safe in a long, long time.

Daniel couldn't get Emma out of his mind all night. That a simple trip into town frightened her continued to haunt him. What must she have endured to be so scared? She told him she'd been brought into police custody and returned to her foster family. He felt an anger boiling up that he knew was wrong. He said a silent prayer to the Lord to calm himself. He found it difficult as he realized that her foster family had hurt her. What had they done to her?

He dozed a few hours before waking well before sunrise. He wanted to talk with Emma, learn the truth. He didn't know why, but he felt protective of her. He would never fight anyone. It wasn't the Amish way, but if someone threatened her, he'd do all he could to ensure she was safe.

With the knowledge that he'd be up well before the rest of his family, Daniel got ready for his day, then quietly went downstairs. He put the coffeepot on the stove and waited for it to perk. He took down several mugs for himself and the rest of his family. He'd drink a quick cup, then take care of the animals before heading over to his aunt and uncle's house to get Emma.

Daniel couldn't see her revealing any more information to him. If he was correct in his thinking, reliving her time with her foster family would be too hard. The coffee finished brewing, and he poured himself a cup, fixing it to his liking. He sat for a moment at the kitchen table sipping coffee, his mind wandering in several directions, consumed with Emma. Today was her third day of work, and according to Henry, she'd been doing well. She had proven trustworthy and hardworking, both traits he valued highly.

Finishing up his coffee, he rose and debated about having another cup. As he reached for the pot, his brother Joseph entered the kitchen. "You're up early."

"*Ja.* Couldn't sleep," Daniel said. "What about you? Something on your mind?"

"Nay. Fell asleep early last night. Thought I'd get a head start on my chores."

"Want coffee first?"

"*Ja.*" Joseph took the filled cup from him.

Daniel poured himself a second cup, then sat down across from his younger brother. "What are you up to today?"

"Thought I'd help *Dat* around the farm. You?"

"Have to take Emma to work, then head over to the construction site."

Joseph stared at him. "Tell me about Emma."

Daniel stiffened. "What about her?"

"What's she like? I heard she was staying with Missy and Arlin."

He nodded. "She is. She's a…" He wasn't sure what to say.

"Some kind of distant cousin, I'm told."

"That's what they say."

"Why do you need to take her to work?" his brother asked.

"She's helping Leah and Henry at their store. I'm trying to help Missy and Arlin."

"That makes sense." Joseph took the last swallow of his coffee and set the mug down. "I'm going to head out to the barn. Take care of the animals."

"You need help?"

"Nay, I can handle it."

The sound of footsteps on the stairs drew their attention. Their little sister Hannah entered the kitchen. Daniel took one long look at her and realized that she wasn't little any more. She was sixteen, an age that worried him.

"Mornin'," Hannah greeted.

"There's coffee," Daniel said, motioning to the coffeepot and mugs on the counter. He watched her nod and fill up a mug.

"I'll see you later, Daniel," Joseph said.

"Ja." He returned his attention back to Hannah. "What are your plans for today?"

"Helping *Mam* with chores."

Daniel breathed a sigh of relief.

"Then I may take a ride into Lancaster," she added, and Daniel nearly groaned.

"You are going there alone?"

"Nay, I thought I'd take Ruth Peachy with me."

His eyes widened. "Why?"

Her eyes gleamed as Hannah lifted her chin. "Because I'm allowed."

The arrival of his parents forestalled any further conversation about his sister's *rumspringa* plans. Daniel looked at the wall clock and realized it was time to pick up Emma.

Minutes later as he pulled onto his uncle's

property, he saw Emma sitting on the stoop, watching as he drove in. He got out of the carriage and approached her.

"Emma, you ready?"

She nodded. "Daniel, I need to talk with you first."

He eyed her with concern. "What's wrong?"

"I can't keep bothering you for a ride. Starting tomorrow, I plan to walk to work."

Daniel shook his head. "Not a *gut* idea, Emma. 'Tis dark until nearly seven forty-five. You don't want to walk when it's dark."

"But it won't be dark when I leave at three. Remember I don't have to be at work until nine. It will be bright by that time."

He still didn't like the idea. What if something happened to her before she made it to the store? Everything inside him wanted to argue with her, but he knew it wouldn't do any good. "Can we talk more about this after work?"

"*Ja*, we can, but my mind is made up and you won't be able to change it."

We'll see, he thought. Somehow, he would convince her that walking to the store wasn't wise. He could talk with his aunt and uncle, see what their thoughts were on Emma's decision. "Where are Missy and Arlin?"

"They left for Meg's an hour ago. Something

about babysitting for Timothy while Meg and Peter head into town for an appointment."

"Do you have your lunch?" he asked.

Emma arched an eyebrow at him. "*Ja.* You?"

He couldn't stop the small smile that cropped up at the sight of her sassy spirit. "*Ja.* Made myself a sandwich last night."

"Let's go, then," she said sharply.

Daniel gazed at her intently. "You're being bossy."

She blushed. "Sorry," she murmured.

Hiding his urge to laugh, Daniel watched as Emma climbed into his buggy unaided before he got in and drove to Yoder's Country Crafts and General Store.

Chapter Eight

Today was Thursday and payday. Henry paid Emma, who refused to take the money. "I owe Leah for the clothes," she said.

"Nay, you don't, Emma," Henry said pleasantly. "Take it. You've earned it. If you won't take your pay, then I'll not have you working at the store. You've made things easier for us. You deserve the little money we can pay you. The garments were a gift."

Emma blinked rapidly as a lump rose in her throat. "Please take it back."

Leah's husband shook his head. "Nay."

She saw the firm resolve in Henry's expression and finally accepted the cash. Henry smiled in approval. Since he and Leah refused to take her money, she'd find another way to repay them. Did he really believe that during her short time working for them she'd made their lives easier? It was true she'd worked alone at the store while Henry had taken Leah to the doctor, but that was nothing compared to what they'd done for her.

Her first purchase from Leah and Henry's store was a wallet. She slipped the remainder of her money inside for safekeeping, then cleaned up the counter. At the end of the workday, Emma realized Daniel hadn't stopped by to check up on her, but he would be coming soon to take her home. The knowledge that she had a little money went a long way in improving her outlook for the future.

Just then, the bells on the front door jingled. Emma's stomach began to flutter as Daniel approached. Would he want to bring up the topic of her walking to work again?

"Are you ready to go?" he asked.

She inclined her head. "I'll tell Henry I'm leaving for the day."

Henry came out from the back room. "*Hallo*, Daniel. Come for Emma?"

"*Ja.*" Daniel locked gazes with her.

"I was just coming to let you know he was here."

Henry smiled at her. "See you tomorrow, Emma."

Emma smiled. "*Ja.*" She glanced at Daniel and saw his thoughtful look. "We should go," she whispered. She followed him out of the store.

He didn't say a word until they were outside in the sunshine. "Emma—"

"I'll be walking to work tomorrow, Daniel. You'll not change my mind." She saw him scowl, but he didn't argue right then, but she knew it was only a matter of time before he did. Emma felt triumphant as she sat back and enjoyed the ride home, until she realized that Daniel wasn't going to accept her decision. Soon, possibly tomorrow, they'd be arguing the safety of her walking to work.

The next morning Emma got ready for work. She would be walking to the store today. She figured it was two, maybe three miles at the most. At least, she hoped so.

"Did you make your lunch?" Missy asked.

"*Ja*, I used some of the chicken salad that was left. That's *oll recht, ja*?"

The older woman smiled. "*Ja*, you can have anything you'd like from the kitchen." She pulled eggs and butter from the refrigerator. "What time is Daniel coming for you?"

"He's not," Emma said. "I told him I'd walk to work this morning."

Missy frowned as she melted butter in a pan

then cracked open the eggs into it. "Do you think that's a *gut* idea?"

"I walked here from Maryland," she told her.

"If you're certain…"

"I'll be fine," Emma assured her. "I don't have to be at work until nine. I'll leave at eight. Once I know how long it will take me, I can adjust my departure time."

Missy nodded, but Emma could see the worry in her expression. "Missy, I can't keep putting Daniel out. He has to work. I know he usually works later than I do, yet he's had to leave early to bring me home."

"I don't think he minds."

Emma wasn't so sure of that. She'd heard what he'd said when she'd been hiding in the barn. He was saving to open a business. The earnings from his current job would finance his future harness shop.

At eight o'clock, Emma grabbed her lunch bag and started to walk in the direction of the store. She hadn't walked far when she heard the sound of buggy wheels behind her. She didn't stop. The carriage drew up next to her, finally snagging her attention.

"Emma." The shock of Daniel's voice halted her.

"What are you doing here, Daniel?" She

continued walking, and he steered his buggy alongside her.

"You wanted to walk so I'm following along beside you to make sure you arrive at the store safely."

She jerked to a stop. "Nay, you're not."

Daniel arched an eyebrow. "*Ja*, I am."

"Daniel—"

"'Tis for the best, Emma. Let me do this, *ja*?"

"But you have to go to work."

"*Ja*, I do, but I'll go in a little late. It will be worth it to know that you reached the store without incident."

"But you've got a business to save up for."

He looked surprised. "And how did you know that?"

"I heard you that first day in the barn." She was across the road from him, but he kept even with her, slowing the horse's pace to hers. "Daniel, you need to go."

"Nay."

She heard a car come up behind her. She turned, saw it was a patrol car and experienced a moment's terror. She kept her head down, hoping the police officer wouldn't stop. He didn't. He seemed to be in a hurry. Fortunately, Daniel had pulled off to the side of the road. He halted the horse and stared at her as if he saw and understood her fear. Once the officer passed, Emma met Daniel's gaze, then closed her eyes briefly before opening them again. "Fine, I'll accept a ride from you, but only because I don't want you to be late for work," she said. Daniel started to get out. "Nay," she warned, "I can get in by myself. 'Tis too dangerous for you to get out and help me. Cars drive past too fast along this road."

Emma climbed into his buggy and settled in the seat. She didn't look at him, and he didn't drive on.

"Emma…"

"We should go."

He sighed before he finally flicked the leathers and drove back onto the road. Minutes later he steered the horse into the store parking lot, close to the hitching post. Daniel didn't say a word. Emma met his gaze, saw emotion in the brown depths of his eyes and felt something swell inside her.

"Daniel…"

"I'm sorry, Emma. I had to follow you," he said before she could continue. "I was worried."

She softened toward him. "That's sweet of you, but—"

"But you no longer need me to take you to and from work," he finished for her.

Emma hesitated. It was true that she didn't need him for transportation, but mostly she was worried about taking advantage of his generosity, especially when he had a job that was important to his future. "*Ja*, although I appreciate the concern." She recalled her reaction to seeing the police cruiser and shuddered.

"My brother Joseph will pick you up at three today," Daniel said. "He works on my *dat*'s farm and he'll be finished well before then."

She didn't like that he'd dictated who she should ride with. She hadn't met Joseph. She didn't want to ride with anyone. "Daniel—"

"Please, Emma."

His soft, imploring tone startled her, and she shot him a glance. How could she resist? "Fine, but today only."

His grin made her breath catch. *"Gut."*

He started to climb down from the buggy. "I can get out on my own," she told him. She knew he was trying to be kind, but she didn't want that. Her feelings about him already confused her.

He nodded, and she could feel his regard as she stepped down from his vehicle. *"Danki*, Daniel."

"I'll see you again sometime soon."

"Ja," she said. Visiting Day was this weekend. She knew she would see him there.

The workday went quickly for Emma. Customers entered the store, buying items for the weekend. She was kept busy helping them find the things they needed.

A quick look at the clock revealed that it was nearly three. Would Daniel's brother come for her as promised?

Minutes later, a young man with dark brown hair and blue eyes entered the store. He smiled as he approached the counter. "Emma," he said, "I'm Joseph."

He was good-looking but in a different way than Daniel. His smile remained on his face as he studied her. It didn't appear as if he felt put out by coming for her. "I'm sorry that you got stuck with me today," she said. "I could have walked home."

Joseph frowned. "I don't think that's a *gut* idea. Besides, I don't mind. 'Tis nice to get out and about."

Leah came out from the back of the store. She'd been up at the house taking a nap. Her blue eyes lit up when she saw Daniel's brother. "Joseph! What a pleasant surprise!"

The young man grinned. He seemed to be close in age to Emma. "I've come to take Emma home."

Leah glanced in her direction. Emma gazed back, trying to keep her thoughts hidden.

"That's nice of you," her friend told Joseph. She turned toward Emma. "I'll see you on Sunday if not before," she said.

Emma only smiled.

"Ready, Emma?" Joseph asked.

"*Ja*. Take care, Leah," she said before she preceded Joseph out of the store.

Unlike Daniel, he didn't offer to help her into his vehicle, a large open carriage with four huge wheels. He simply untied his horse from the hitching post as Emma climbed into the high seat. Joseph got in. Emma held on tight as the carriage lurched as he flicked the leathers before he steered the horse onto the road.

He was quiet as he drove toward the Stoltzfus house. Finally, he turned to her. "How old are you?" he asked.

Emma looked at him, trying to figure out why it was important for him to know. How much of her background was he told?

"Seventeen," she murmured.

Joseph smiled. "I'm eighteen." He returned his attention to the road. "So, you're a cousin of *Endie* Missy."

Emma didn't know what to say and realized he'd been told only her cover story. "*Ja*."

"First time visiting Happiness?"

"*Ja.* My parents are gone, and I have no *bruders* or sisters."

He studied her briefly with concern. "I'm sorry."

She smiled. "Don't be. I'm fine. Besides, they are with the Lord now, *ja*?" She hoped so, anyway. Her parents had been labeled sinners. She prayed that God had taken them home to reside in heaven with Him.

The house rose up on the left. Joseph made the turn and pulled up by the side door. Missy was taking clothes down from the line. Emma frowned. "I told her I'd help with those."

"Then 'tis a *gut* thing I brought you home," Joseph said with good humor.

She saw the teasing twinkle in his eyes and decided she liked Daniel's younger brother. "I appreciate the ride."

"You're most *willkomm*. Shall I pick you up Monday after work?"

"I don't want to impose. If I haven't made other arrangements, I'll let you know."

The young man nodded.

Emma went to the clothesline. "Missy, I'll help with this. I'm not doing enough chores," she said.

Missy glanced at her. "You do more than enough, Emma." Her gaze went beyond her. "Joseph!"

Emma was surprised to see that Joseph had followed her. "I couldn't leave without saying *hallo*," he said. "I'm the one who brought Emma home today."

Missy looked from one to the other. "That was nice of you."

"Daniel insisted," Emma muttered.

"It was my pleasure," Joseph assured her with a smile.

Emma began to unpin the remaining garments from the clothesline. She ignored the conversation between aunt and nephew. When she was done, despite Missy's protests, she picked up the wicker laundry basket and took it inside the house. Missy followed moments later.

"'Tis important for me to help," Emma said.

Missy looked at her with a soft expression. "You help out plenty. But you can help me cook for Visiting Day if you'd like."

She nodded. "*Danki.* I'll be happy to."

The next morning she and Missy baked the upside-down chocolate cake, one of Missy's well-known and sought-after specialties, and a number of pies. Emma enjoyed working with the pie crust, kneading it on a floured table, then rolling it out into two circles. She made an apple pie first.

"The apples this time of year are fresh and

crisp," Missy told her. "Perfect for pie making as well as eating."

"It smells delicious," Emma said with a grin.

"I'll teach you to make a shoofly pie next." Missy smiled at her. She wore a quilted apron tied around her waist. She gave one to Emma, which she quickly donned. Both aprons had been handmade by Missy.

"What is shoofly pie?"

"It's thick and sugary and delicious. We call it shoofly because if set on the windowsill to cool, flies swarm around it eager for a taste."

Emma wrinkled her nose. "Eww."

Missy laughed. "Don't worry. We won't let that happen."

By late afternoon, she and Missy had made not only cake and pies but four loaves of bread, macaroni salad and a roast beef. "We don't do any cooking or housework on Sundays, Emma." She pulled the roast beef from the oven and set it on a hot mat on the worktable. "As I explained earlier, tomorrow we'll have visitors. It's not a church service day but a day when family and friends get together to enjoy one another's company. My sister-in-law and her family will be coming. So will Leah and my other daughters. It should be a nice day."

Emma was nervous. Would she be able to act like she belonged? How much did the family know about her background? Daniel knew and so did Leah, Charlie and Ellie. But what of the others? Of Leah's sisters Meg and Nell? She hoped and prayed that she fit in well enough that everyone would accept her as one of them.

Sunday morning Emma got up and dressed in clean garments before she rolled and pinned her hair, then covered it with a white prayer *kapp*. Their visitors would be coming at 10:00 a.m., Missy had told her the day before. It was seven now, later than usual for her to rise. She descended the stairs and found Missy in the kitchen setting out muffins and jam for breakfast.

"I'm going to feed the animals," Emma told her.

Missy shook her head. "Arlin got a head start. The animals are taken care of."

Emma flushed guiltily. "Where's Jeremiah?"

As if recognizing his name, the family dog lifted his head from his dog bed in the corner of the room.

"Ah, there you are!" Emma exclaimed. "Would you like to go for a walk?" She grabbed his leash and the dog ran toward her, eager to be outdoors. "Let's go, then."

She took him across the yard, waiting a minute for him to do his business before she took him into the barn. Arlin was inside watching his horses eat with their noses deep in their feed buckets. "Good morning, Arlin."

The man turned and smiled at her. "Mornin', Emma."

"I'm sorry I overslept."

"You needed your rest." The warmth of his expression relaxed her.

"I hope you don't mind that I brought Jeremiah with me."

The man smiled affectionately at his dog. "Nay. I'm sure he was ready for a stroll."

"Missy said that breakfast will be ready in a few minutes."

"I'll head over, then, and wash up." He started toward the door.

"Arlin."

He turned to her with raised eyebrows.

"Danki," she said softly.

"Nothing to be thanked for, Emma. You're always welcome in our *haus*."

Emma felt overwhelmed with emotion as she accompanied Arlin on the walk back. As she entered the kitchen, she felt her mouth water. She was hungry, tempted by the fresh muffins on the table accompanied by several jars of jams and jellies. Since she'd moved in with the Amish couple, she'd been well fed. Just shy of a week, she was already feeling stronger than when she'd first arrived. And this simple breakfast, she thought, was only the start of a day that would be filled with food and fellowship.

The day was unseasonably warm but not humid. After breakfast, Missy and Emma opened all the windows to let the fresh air into the house. Emma was pouring glasses of cold tea when she heard the sound of buggy wheels on the dirt driveway. The first of their visitors had arrived. She picked up a glass and went to the window as a gray family buggy pulled in near the barn.

She waited with bated breath to see who was in the vehicle, expecting—and hoping— it would be Daniel. A man she hadn't met before climbed out, then helped the others get down. A woman with a baby stepped out with his assistance, followed by a little boy, who was lifted into his father's arms. They headed toward the house. Emma opened the door as they approached. The man froze a moment as he saw her before he continued his approach with his wife and baby.

"*Gut* mornin'," she greeted. Her heart raced as she held the door open for them to enter.

"You must be Emma," the woman said. "I'm Sarah Lapp. This is Jedidiah, my husband, and these two are our children."

"Jed," he invited. "I'm Daniel's brother." The man studied her thoughtfully.

The mention of Daniel's name gave her an odd little thrill until she began to wonder how much of the truth Daniel had told his family about her.

The man smiled. "You're a cousin from out of state, I hear. *Willkomm*."

She hid her discomfort at the necessary deception. She managed to smile. "I'm grateful that Missy and Arlin put up with my company."

"I'm sure they love having you here."

"We do," Missy said as she entered the room. "Jed, Sarah, I'm glad you could join us today."

Jed's expression softened. "Wouldn't miss a visit with my favorite *endie* and *onkel*."

Missy laughed. "You're a charmer like your *bruders*." She reached for the baby in his arms.

"Noah and Rachel can't make it," Sarah said. "Susanna is sick, and they thought it best to keep her home."

"Poor girl. I hope she feels better soon," Missy said.

"Isaac and Ellen won't be coming either," Jed added. "They're with Ellen's *eldre* today."

Missy nodded. "Leah and Henry will be over later after a brief visit to Ellen's parents."

She explained to Emma, "Isaac is married to Ellen. Henry and my nephew Isaac are best friends."

"Ellie and Reuben will be here any minute with Ethan." Missy paused. "Meg, Peter and Timothy are with Horseshoe Joe and Miriam today."

An open carriage pulled in, and two couples and a child got out. "Charlie and Nate," Missy said with a grin of satisfaction. "And Ellie, Reuben and Ethan."

Another vehicle entered the property moments later. Jed grinned. "My *mudder* and *vadder*." Emma waited patiently beside Missy while Jed approached the family buggy and opened the door for his parents and siblings.

"Daniel, Joseph and Hannah are with them," Sarah said.

"Where's Elijah?" Jed asked as his family entered the small home.

"He and Martha are at the Masts'," Daniel said. His gaze locked with Emma's, and she felt a fluttering within her chest.

She reluctantly pulled her eyes away from him. "May I get anyone something to drink?" she asked everyone. She held up her cup. "Iced tea?"

Sarah, Jed and Hannah wanted some.

"I'll help," Ellie said. "Reuben?"

The man smiled at her lovingly. *"Ja."*

"I'll have some as well," Joseph said.

"I'll get it," Hannah said.

Emma grabbed a few plastic cups and poured tea for those who wanted it. Daniel entered the house, carrying a large bowl in each arm. His sister Hannah followed him inside.

"I'll help," Hannah said. The girl had pretty blue eyes and blond hair. Emma saw the resemblance between Daniel and his sister in the shape of their eyes. She handed two cups to Hannah.

Daniel placed the bowls of food on the kitchen counter. He watched Emma fill two more glasses with iced tea. Emma gave them to him. *"Danki,"* he murmured as he held her gaze.

She rewarded him a small smile and breathed easier as he carried them outside. She took another pitcher from the refrigerator and filled four more cups, which she set on the counter.

"Thank the Lord 'tis a nice enough day to eat outside," Ellie said with a smile. "This *haus* is too small for all these people." She grabbed two of the cups and left the house.

Despite Ellie's belief, Emma secretly thought the house perfect for any number of people, as Missy and Arlin filled it with love for their family and friends.

Daniel returned. "I thought there might be more," he said, reaching around her for the two plastic cups. His nearness made her heart rate spike. He stepped back but didn't move. His eyes warmed as his lips curved. "Emma, earlier you didn't say *hallo* to me." He looked amused. "I'll say it first, then. *Hallo*, Emma. Nice to see you."

"*Hallo*, Daniel." She blushed. "I should go out and see if anyone wants something other than tea." Without waiting for his response, she brushed by him and exited the house. She was aware of him following close behind her. She asked around, but no one else needed anything. She went back into the house. To her surprise, Daniel followed her inside.

"I need to take Jeremiah for a walk," she murmured as she grabbed his leash and headed toward the barn. Arlin had put the dog in the barn so that the animal wasn't overwhelmed with all the company. Inside the barn, she went to Jeremiah's stall. Arlin had supplied his pet with plenty of creature comforts—his bed, some chew toys, a bowl of water and one of dry dog food.

"Hey, boy," she whispered as she unlatched the stall door and went inside, then closed it behind her. Emma approached the little dog and crouched down to pet him. "Are you lonely in here, buddy?" she asked as she ran her fingers through his fur. She laughed when Jeremiah flipped onto his back for her to rub his belly.

"You have a kind owner," she said softly. "You're lucky." She grinned. "Missy and Arlin love you." She sighed. "I do, too." She continued to stroke the dog's belly. "Want to go for a walk? We can walk through the fields toward the back road. What do you think?"

"I don't think that would be a *gut* idea," a familiar voice said.

She gasped and looked up to see Daniel leaning over the half door.

"You left in a hurry," he said. "Has it been that long since Jeremiah went out last?"

Emma blushed. She'd taken him for a walk less than two hours ago. But she needed the comfort Jeremiah gave her. Everyone had been so kind to her, but she reminded herself that she was only living here temporarily, and she felt guilty and out of place. Daniel's expression was unreadable as he studied her.

"Does it matter when he was out last?" she asked, her tone crisp.

"Maybe. What if Missy needs your help?"

"Oh, I…" Embarrassment made her look away. "I can tie him outside and keep him from being underfoot. He'd like watching everyone, and he won't make a pest of himself."

She clipped on Jeremiah's leash. This man did something to her. She was attracted to him although he made her feel off-kilter.

Daniel stepped aside to make room for her and Jeremiah to exit the stall. She took the dog out into the yard, aware of Daniel behind her.

Missy was in the yard chatting with three women. It didn't look like Missy needed help. Emma flashed Daniel an accusing look, but he merely arched an eyebrow at her.

She approached Missy and her friends. "Emma," Missy greeted with a smile. "Come and meet my sister-in-law Katie."

She was suddenly the focus of three kind gazes. *"Hallo,"* Emma murmured. She recognized Katie Lapp, Daniel's mother, in the similarity of her features with Daniel's.

"'Tis nice to meet you," Emma said.

Katie smiled. "Daniel has talked about you."

Emma stilled. "Nothing bad, I hope."

The woman shook her head. "All *gut*. And Leah and Henry have said nothing but nice things about you. I've been told you're a hard worker, and your help at the store allows my niece to get off her feet and rest."

Relaxing, Emma gave her a genuine smile. "I enjoy helping Leah and working at the store."

"I'm glad you like working there," Missy

said. "Leah will need you more in the coming weeks."

"Ja," Katie agreed. "She'll be tired. I remember when I carried Jacob and Elijah. My twin sons," she explained. "I was exhausted by noon every day."

"Henry urges Leah to nap in the afternoon. She didn't want to at first, but now she gets so tired that she listens to him when he urges her to go up to the house and lie down."

"Are you taking Jeremiah for a walk?" Missy asked.

"I thought I would tie him up outside away from everyone. Unless you think it would be better if I put him in my room."

Missy nodded. "That might be a better idea."

Emma excused herself to take Jeremiah upstairs to her room. She took off his leash, then refilled the bowl of water for him, setting it next to the makeshift bed she'd made for him.

When Emma returned downstairs, the women were gathering food from the kitchen to take outside. She grabbed a large bowl that Daniel had carried in earlier and took it to the table that Arlin had set up outside for food. The men had also set up tables made from plywood laid across sawhorses. Kitchen chairs had been brought outside for people to sit on. Everyone else searched for a comfortable place to sit. When it was time to eat, Emma filled her plate and sat on the small stoop near the side door of the house.

Watching Missy's family interact from a distance, Emma saw the love among family members. She experienced an intense longing to belong in some way. She sat and silently ate from her plate with her cup of lemonade next to her on the step.

Daniel came over to her, and she tensed. "Mind if I sit down?" he asked.

She shook her head and moved her glass of lemonade to her other side, shifting over to give him room.

He sat close beside her, and she struggled to appear at ease.

"The food is delicious."

Emma managed to smile. "*Ja*, I especially like the salads your mother made."

The air grew tense with silence.

"Did you have a *gut* first week?" Daniel asked.

"Daniel—"

"'Tis a simple question, Emma."

She faced him, found him studying her with an intensity that startled her. "*Ja*, it was a *gut* week. I learned a lot from Leah and Henry."

He nodded, then went back to eating. "Was

it a problem for you to have Joseph to bring you home yesterday?"

"Nay." She took a sip from her lemonade.

"Then you won't mind if he comes to take you home every day."

"Daniel—"

"I'll take you to work and he can bring you home."

She sighed. "I don't think so."

He scowled at her. "What? Why not?"

Something about his tone made her breath catch. "I don't want to bother either of you."

"You won't be bothering us. We offered."

"It doesn't seem right."

"But we *want* to help," he said, his expression sincere.

Her heart melted. "I'll accept your help for now," she said, "until I can make other arrangements."

His grin warmed her heart. "That's fine."

Daniel surprised her by staying close to her for a time. Emma found that she didn't mind his company as much as she thought she would. He was entertaining as he told her stories about each of his relatives. "Charlie used to be a wild child," he said.

"Charlie?"

"*Ja*. Nate didn't know what to make of her until she convinced him she was perfect for him."

Emma chuckled as Daniel smiled at her.

A short time later, he excused himself to discuss something with his brothers. Emma headed toward Missy and Katie, who stood talking with Leah and Ellie in the shade of an oak tree.

"I tell you 'tis a shame," Missy said. "David knows better. No technology. 'Tis against the Ordnung. 'Tis no wonder the elders want him to be shunned."

"The bishop believes 'tis the right thing to do," Katie Lapp said.

"David understands our rules and what's expected of him."

Overhearing, Emma froze, waiting to hear more. They were about to shun someone? In this community? She suddenly felt sick to her stomach.

"David says he found it, whatever it is. I think it's a tablet. He works in a supermarket in Lancaster. His sister said he bought it."

"And it runs on electricity," Katie pointed out.

"And I heard he plugs it in to charge it at Whittier's Store. Bob Whittier has some code that David puts into the tablet so that he can view the English world on it," Leah said.

"He clearly doesn't think he did anything wrong," Leah's sister Ellie added.

"Bishop John spoke with David and he's not sorry for owning one."

Emma stepped closer, needing to know more.

"Emma!" Sarah Lapp exclaimed. "Come and join us."

Her heart fluttered in her chest. If these people ever learned the truth about her shunned family, she'd be ostracized like they planned to do to this David. "I didn't mean to intrude."

"You're not," Katie assured her with a smile. "We were chatting about a member of our community who has gone against the Ordnung. 'Tis a terrible thing. Our bishop and church elders have decided that he should be shunned, especially since the man feels no remorse for what he's done."

Emma nodded as tension rose within her. "If he were sorry, would he still be shunned?"

"If he said he regretted what he did—and meant it—then he would be accepted back into our community," Missy said. "Shunning is simply the Amish way of tough love. David Fisher can remain in Happiness, but no one will sit or eat with him. Nor will members of the community do business with him."

"I see." And Emma truly understood for the first time about shunning. One had to do a terrible wrong to be shunned. She realized she never really understood what shunning—or ostracizing a person—meant. Only that her parents told her that they could never return to their Amish community. Never see her grandparents, other relatives and friends. Now she knew that if they had, her family would have rejected them.

I shouldn't stay. As much as she would have liked to, she didn't truly belong here.

When it was time for everyone to leave, Emma watched Daniel and his family climb into their buggies. His hands holding the leathers, Daniel saw her and smiled. She eyed him warily, then turned away, unable to bear the thought of his rejection should he learn the truth about her.

In a few weeks, she'd turn eighteen. She wasn't sure where she'd go, but she knew she had to leave now. She couldn't stay. She would work one more day and pay for the clothes that Leah had provided for her. Then she would leave Happiness and the Amish community here. *And Daniel.* She would never forget any of them. And she'd always remember Daniel and how kind he'd been to her. It would hurt to go, but if he ever learned the truth about her, she was sure he'd reject her.

That would be more painful than anything her foster father had done.

Chapter Nine

Daniel arrived at the house the next morning as Emma pinned the last of the wet laundry on the clothesline. She heard the sound of wheels on the dirt driveway and turned to see him climb out of his buggy and head toward the house. Aware that he hadn't seen her, she approached the house and entered within seconds of Daniel's entry.

"*Hallo*, Daniel," she said.

He eyed her with surprise. "You were outside?"

"*Ja*. I was at the clothesline."

Missy handed her a paper bag. "I made you lunch."

"*Danki*," she said solemnly. She grabbed her sweater from a wall hook. It was chilly outside, and the temperature would likely drop later in the day.

She was quiet as Daniel drove her to work. Her throat felt tight as she stared through the side window. She could barely swallow. She was saddened by the realization that today would be the last time she would see or spend time with him.

The Yoders' store loomed ahead on the right side of the road. Daniel steered his horse to the parking lot. He sat a moment without a word until Emma started to get out.

He caught her by the hand to stop her. "Emma, wait," he said.

She stiffened.

"Something is bothering you," he said.

"I'm fine."

He shook his head. "Nay, you're not. We had a nice day yesterday, *ja*? Then at some point, something changed and you seemed upset. You became quiet."

"Daniel, I'm fine."

He studied her for a long time. There was something in his expression that made her heart race. "You'd tell me if you were upset?"

Emma shifted uncomfortably. She didn't want to have this conversation. He seemed genuinely concerned about her, which only made her feel more guilty and sad. "You need to get to work, and I should get inside. Leah and Henry are waiting for me."

He inclined his head. "Joseph will bring you home this afternoon."

"Oll recht." She got out of the vehicle but paused at the front entrance of the store. "Take care, Daniel Lapp."

He frowned. "I'll see you tomorrow morning, Emma."

Despite her decision to leave, Emma experienced an odd warmth in her chest from Daniel's concern for her. She entered the store and approached the counter. *"Gut* morning," she greeted the Yoders.

"Gut morning, Emma," Leah said, and Henry smiled.

"Should I restock shelves today?"

"Leah has another doctor's appointment," Henry told her. "Can you handle the store for us?"

"Ja, I'd be happy to."

Henry smiled. *"Danki.* I'll carry out some boxes for you."

She quickly hurried to the door that led to the back room. "I'll manage."

The man started to object.

"If it's canned goods or jars, you can carry them for me. But I'll start with the lighter items." Emma brought out a number of boxes and set them in the corner to grab when she needed them.

The morning passed quickly. Henry left with Leah for the doctor's appointment at noon, and with them gone Emma chose that time to pay for the garments Leah had given her. She opened the register drawer and put in a hundred dollars. The rest she would need if she didn't want to find herself living on the streets again.

The front door opened with a tinkling of bells as Joseph Lapp stepped into the store. Flushing with guilt, Emma slammed shut the drawer and smiled at him. "Joseph, is it that time already?"

"Ja." He didn't return her smile. "Are you ready to go?"

She stared at him. Something felt wrong. She looked away. "Let me lock the doors and we can slip out the back." Emma brushed by him on the way to lock the front door.

"Where are Leah and Henry?"

"Leah had a doctor's appointment."

Joseph nodded. He watched her lock the front door, then waited while she grabbed her wallet from under the counter. He followed her out through the back of the store. After ensuring that the rear door was locked, she faced Daniel's brother.

"You didn't have to come to take me home."

He narrowed his gaze. "Why not?" He

opened his mouth as if he wanted to say something else, then promptly shut it.

Emma followed him to his buggy, then climbed in. Joseph got situated in the seat next to her and picked up the leathers. He sat a moment without moving. Finally, he turned and met her gaze. "Tell me that you didn't take money out of the register."

Emma gaped at him in shock. "I didn't take money out of the register."

"Then why did you open it? There were no customers in the store."

She blinked back tears. "I didn't take money from the register," she insisted.

He stared at her. She faced him with glistening eyes. "I put money *in* the drawer," she admitted hoarsely, her throat tight. "Leah won't take any payment for the dresses she gave me. I needed to repay her, so I thought I'd—"

"Slip it in the register when she wasn't here?" Joseph said softly.

"*Ja.*"

She braced herself for his response, but he just smiled at her. "Let's go. I'm sure you're tired and ready to go home." He believed her, she realized.

Emma nodded. She wished the Stoltzfus residence was truly her home. But it wasn't, and it never would be. So she would leave tonight.

She settled her wallet in her lap and hugged herself. Despite her sweater, she was cold. The temperature had cooled, and there was a hint of dampness in the air. The distant sky was dark, as if threatening rain.

Joseph noticed the change in temperature and the dark sky as well. "I need to get you home before it pours."

"Will you be *oll recht*?" she asked with concern. "Or will you stay with us until the rain passes?"

"I don't live too far. I'm sure I'll make it home before the storm hits."

It had started to drizzle by the time Joseph drove his wagon onto his uncle's property.

"Are you sure you won't stay?" Emma asked.

He gave her a genuine smile that warmed her inside. His willingness to believe her about the register meant a lot to her.

Emma climbed out of his vehicle and waved to him as he drove away before she ran to the house. She burst into the kitchen. "A storm's coming."

"I saw," Missy said. "Thank the Lord you're home." The woman eyed her damp garments. "You're shivering, child. Take off your sweater. Tea? It will warm you up."

"*Ja.*" She would miss these moments with

Missy. She would miss her and Arlin and their married daughters and family. And the Lapps. But she'd miss Daniel most of all.

As she spooned sugar into her tea, Emma thought about leaving. Should she leave at night? Or in the morning? She wouldn't go in the rain. She'd get sick if she did. If she became ill and out of sorts, the police would have a better chance of finding her.

She'd have to plan her departure wisely. She was safe here until someone learned the truth about her identity and her past. Then she'd be shunned and tossed out of Happiness. She wished there were a way to work at the Yoders' store for a little longer so she could save a bit more money for food and shelter until she could figure out what to do next.

"Emma." Missy's urgent calling of her name alerted her to the woman's concern that she'd said Emma's name several times without a response. "What's wrong?"

Emma shook her head. "Nothing. I'm fine."

The older woman looked as if she didn't believe her, which made Emma feel all the more guilty. Emma remembered well the ideals of her Amish community, and she knew that she rarely thought much about going against them. Until now. Because of Missy and Arlin and Leah and the others. Until Daniel.

"May I help you prepare supper?" Emma asked, hoping to distract her.

"We're having leftovers. You can help me make a dessert if you'd like."

Emma grinned. "What will we have?"

"I thought we'd make custard."

"Sounds delicious." Emma put thoughts of leaving from her mind for now and concentrated on spending the rest of the day with the woman who had come to mean so much to her. Her thoughts continually remained on all she'd be leaving behind when she left.

Daniel and his construction crew stopped work early because of the rain. He climbed into his buggy and headed home. Joseph would have taken Emma home by now. He thought of her too often lately. Why? It wasn't as if he could wed her. The fact that she looked as if she fit into his Amish community didn't negate the knowledge that she was an Englisher who would soon leave.

He'd had a good week at work. Next week would prove to be better, moneywise. He had saved a lot of his pay. It was time for him to look for a place to rent for his upcoming business. What if all the places he liked were more expensive than he'd anticipated?

Instead of going straight home, he decided

to drive through the area to see if there were any locations that might work for him. The ideal spot would have a house and a decent outbuilding he could use as his harness shop. He thought of Emma again as he passed by some houses with outbuildings. What would she think of the homes in the area? Would she come with him to look at places if he asked? He wasn't sure what was for sale. He would have to ask around or contact a real estate agent. He might have to rent first, but he really wanted to buy a place.

He gave up after a half hour and steered his horse toward home.

Daniel drove onto his father's property and pulled the buggy close to the barn. He undid the horse and took him to his stall. After he fed and watered him, he took care of the rest of the animals before he headed in.

His *mam* was in the kitchen making supper. His father sat at the kitchen table with a steaming cup of coffee before him. They both looked over as he came in. *"Hallo."*

"Daniel," his mother greeted.

Then he turned his attention to his father. "Did you get what you wanted done today, *Dat?*"

Samuel Lapp nodded. *"Ja,* Joseph and I worked on the new outbuilding we started."

"Do you want to work on it tonight?" He couldn't take off from his job, but he could work on it after hours.

"No need. Another day's work is all we need."

"I took care of the animals," Daniel said. "What's for supper?"

"Can't you smell it?" his mother teased.

"Fried chicken." Daniel loved fried chicken. Did Emma know how to make it? he wondered.

"With mashed potatoes and green beans."

He grinned. "My favorite. Any coffee left?" When his mother nodded, he took a mug from the cabinet and filled it. He sat next to his father and fixed his coffee. "Where's Joseph?"

"Upstairs washing up."

"Did he take Emma home?"

Samuel shrugged. "He said he did."

As if on cue, Joseph entered the kitchen, his hair wet and in freshly laundered clothes. "Said he did what?" he asked.

"Take Emma home."

Joseph nodded. "*Ja.* Got her there before the rain hit hard."

"I appreciate it."

"Did she give you any trouble?"

"*Nay*, but—" His brother's brow furrowed. "Would you come outside with me for a minute?" He shot his parents a quick look."

Daniel frowned. "Is something wrong?"

"Not really, but there is something I'd like to discuss."

He followed Joseph onto the covered front porch. "What's so important that we can't talk about it in front of *Mam* and *Dat*?"

"'Tis about Emma."

Daniel chest tightened. "What about her?"

"When I went to get her, I caught her in the cash drawer." Joseph paused. "There were no customers in the store. I asked her if she had taken anything."

"If she was stealing money?"

Joseph nodded. "*Ja*. She denied it. Said she was putting money in the drawer because Leah and Henry won't let her pay for the garments Leah gave her. Daniel, I believe she's telling the truth, but I wanted you to know." There was concern for Emma in his expression. "I feel terrible for questioning her like she was a thief. I don't really know her so I had to ask." He met Daniel's gaze directly. "She had tears in her eyes, Daniel. She was hurt that I doubted her innocence."

Daniel listened, unsure what to think. "I appreciate that you told me." Daniel wanted to trust Emma, but like his *bruder*, he would have questioned her. Still, he wanted to believe her, so he would until she proved herself a liar.

"I think she'll tell you. She was really upset."

Daniel could only nod. "We'd better go in before *Dat* comes looking for us." He managed to smile. "I'm hungry."

Joseph grinned. "I'm starving."

Daniel's mind was on Emma as they went back into the house. He hated the idea that she might have stolen from Leah and Henry. It made more sense that she'd tried to pay for the clothes that Leah gave her. It probably bothered Emma not to give back what she felt she owed the Yoders.

The young woman fit in well with his community. What if it was all an act on her part? She was English, and Englishers could be deceitful. *Everyone is human and capable of deceit.* He was upset at the thought that Emma could deceive any of them.

After dinner, he could go to see his *onkel* and *endie* and visit for a spell. Arlin was like a second father to him, so it wasn't unusual for him to drop by uninvited.

He'd also get to visit with Emma, too. Daniel felt a burst of happiness as he pictured her living in his community, in his home, having his children…

She's an Englisher. She will never stay.

Daniel sighed. He had to confront her, make her tell the truth about whether or not she'd taken money from the store register. And what if she didn't? *I'll have to apologize for asking.*

He didn't want her to be guilty of stealing. He appreciated how hard she worked for his aunt and uncle, and for Leah and Henry. *She has no family. Is she happy here?*

He didn't need the distraction of his growing feelings for her. He needed to concentrate on getting his harness shop up and running.

"*Soohn*, you seem pensive. Are you *oll recht*?" his mother asked as he sat at the kitchen table.

"Just thinking about work," he said.

"Work?" his father teased. "Or the business you want to open?"

Daniel smiled. "The business," he confessed.

"I have some money set aside," *Dat* began.

"Nay, *Dat*, I need to do this on my own."

"There is no shame in accepting a little help when you need it," Samuel insisted. "You can pay me back once you're established and earning a good living."

Daniel regarded his father thoughtfully. "I'll keep that in mind."

His father nodded approvingly. "*Gut.*"

Joseph took the seat across from him. The only one missing from the table was his sister. "Where is Hannah?" Daniel asked.

"She's visiting Rose Ann," his *mam* said. "But I expected her back by now."

Samuel frowned. "I should look for her."

"I'll look for her after supper," Daniel said.

"She's old enough for *rumspringa*," Joseph pointed out.

Though Daniel knew that, he was as concerned as his *mam* and *dat*.

A sound at the door drew their attention, then Hannah bounced in, smiling. Her eyes widened as she saw that her family was already seated for supper. "I'm sorry I'm late. I lost track of time."

"We just sat down," his mother said, looking relieved.

"Gut." Hannah seemed reassured.

"Come and eat." Daniel motioned to the empty chair.

"I'll wash my hands first." She walked over to the kitchen sink. "What's for dinner?"

"If you'd been here—" her father growled.

"Samuel," Katie said gently. "Would you pass the fried chicken, please?"

Hannah dried her hands with a kitchen towel, then sat in her usual seat, on Daniel's right. "Smells delicious. You're right, *Mam*. I should have been here to help," she said sincerely. "I won't be late again."

"'Tis fine, *dochter*," their *mudder* said. "You can help me with tomorrow night's supper."

Daniel observed his family while he ate. He felt warm and comfortable with them. Emma didn't have a family who made her feel that way. Had she ever? he wondered. He silently groaned. Why couldn't he stop thinking about her?

He thought of postponing his visit, but he wanted to see Emma this evening. To see Emma? Or Arlin and Missy? He'd visit with his relatives *and* Emma, he decided.

Chapter Ten

The scent of vanilla wafted in the air, teasing her taste buds, as Emma learned to make custard. "It smells delicious."

"'Tis one of my favorite desserts," Missy admitted.

"What else can I help with?"

"You can take the ham and the sweet-and-sour green beans out of the refrigerator," the older woman said. "Then would you check on Arlin? He's been in his workshop for most the day."

"Okay. Should I set the table first?"

Missy smiled. *"Ja, danki."*

Emma put out plates, then placed the food in the center of the table. When she was done, she walked to the barn to where Arlin kept a small workshop in the far back corner. He liked to build birdhouses and other small wooden items. Missy had told her earlier that Arlin had started his woodworking to earn extra money to pay off medical bills after their daughter Meg had been hospitalized with a serious illness. Their Amish community, which was in Ohio at the time, had given them financial help, but Arlin had been determined to do what he could to pay off some of the bills himself. While doing so, he'd discovered he enjoyed making things, so now he did it for the joy of it rather than necessity.

Emma entered the barn and approached Arlin at his workbench. He was sawing a block of wood with a handsaw. The scent of slightly burnt wood lingered in the air. As she studied Arlin before he knew she was there, she blinked back tears. She would miss him and Missy. She had to go, but she would be leaving a huge section of her heart behind.

Arlin set down his saw and picked up a piece of sandpaper. As he sanded the newly cut wooden edges, Emma shifted closer. "Busy, I see," she said softly so she wouldn't startle him.

He smiled at her. He didn't seem in the least surprised to see her, as if he knew she'd been there all along. "Come and take a look at what I've been making."

Emma leaned closer to see a small wooden

box, which was beautifully handcrafted. She saw that the lid opened and closed on tiny brass hinges. "It's lovely."

"I'm glad you like it," Arlin said. "I made it for you."

She gasped. "For me?"

"Ja." The man had affection in his gaze as he handed it to her.

"'Tis the most wonderful thing I've ever seen," she breathed as she cradled the box lovingly in her hands. "I've never had anything this nice before." She swallowed against a tight throat. *"Danki."*

"You are most *willkomm, dochter.*"

Her eyes filled with tears. He had called her daughter. She turned away before he could see them. "Missy said to tell you that supper's ready."

"I'll be in shortly," he promised, his voice soft.

She nodded, then quickly headed to the house, holding her precious gift. She let out a sob halfway there and paused to wipe her tears and get control of her emotions. She was leaving. She didn't want to go, but she knew she couldn't stay. This Amish community practiced shunning, and the knowledge urged her to leave town before they learned the truth about her.

She'd have to write a note to soften the blow and thank them. She would confess that her time with them, as short as it was, had been the best time of her life. She would go, and she would take this handmade box with her, a memory of when she'd been regarded as a daughter by a kind man and his wife.

Emma entered the kitchen, showed Missy what Arlin had made for her, then took it to her room, where it would stay for only a few hours more. Then she went downstairs and joined Missy and Arlin at the supper table, where she pretended that everything was fine. Her heart was breaking as she smiled and ate supper, and then as she helped Missy clean the dishes and put them away afterward. She was about to plead tiredness and head up to her room when a knock on the side door stopped her. Seconds later, Daniel greeted them as he let himself in.

"I'd like to take Emma for a ride while there is still a hint of sunlight," he said. "We won't be gone long." He locked gazes with her. "Emma?"

Because she cared for him, she agreed. "I'll get my sweater," she said, and went to retrieve it from her room. She wanted—needed—to spend a little more time in his company before she left. She heard him talking with his uncle as she reached the bottom stair landing.

"I thought I'd take Emma for ice cream at Whittier's. Do you want any?"

She couldn't hear what Arlin said. She entered the room, and his uncle was smiling, so he must be fine with Daniel's plans.

Daniel met her gaze. "Do you like ice cream?" he asked.

"*Ja*, of course." It felt like there was something more beneath Daniel's invitation. If this wasn't strictly a social call, then what was it? Had Joseph told him what he'd seen earlier today? Would Daniel believe her innocent or guilty of stealing from the Yoders?

Suddenly, it was important to her that she and Daniel be on good terms when she left.

Daniel reached his carriage before her. This vehicle was open with two large wheels to support the body, which had only enough room for two to sit in. Was it a courting buggy? From what she remembered, Amish couples courted in secret until they decided they were ready for the next step. That was when a young Amish man would approach the bishop with his intentions. The bishop would then reach out to the girl's family to gain permission on behalf of the young man for them to wed.

She didn't realize she'd stopped by the carriage, frozen in place, until Daniel lifted her into the buggy with his hands at her waist. Her heart thumped wildly. She didn't know what to make of his evening visit, but she had a bad feeling it wasn't because he wanted to buy her an ice cream.

Daniel felt Emma's tension as he settled into the seat next to her. He turned to her. "What kind of ice cream do you like?"

She shrugged without looking at him. "I like all kinds," she murmured.

He kept his tone light. "Favorite flavor?"

Emma met his gaze then. They hadn't left the property, and he wouldn't until she answered his question. He searched her pretty brown eyes for any clue to what she was thinking and found nothing except perhaps sadness. The realization floored him. "Chocolate chip mint," she breathed.

He laughed. "Mine, too."

She beamed at him, her happiness stealing his breath away.

"Let's go get some," he said. He flicked the reins and headed the buggy toward the road. A quick glance at the house showed his aunt and uncle standing at the window. When they saw he had caught sight of them, they waved and grinned, then disappeared.

Daniel suddenly felt lighthearted as he drove the short distance to Whittier's Store. He was spending time with Emma. He liked being with her. He pushed the thought of her stealing from his mind. She might tell him on his own. Joseph believed her. But then why did his brother tell him what he'd seen? In case she mentioned it, Joseph had said. And if she didn't?

He focused on her sitting beside him, on the way the light breeze teased the tendrils of her hair that escaped from beneath her prayer *kapp*. Whittier's Store loomed ahead. Owned by Bob Whittier, an Englisher, it was a frequent stop for many in his community. He wondered if Emma had ever visited, but one look at her face showed him that she hadn't.

Daniel pulled up to the hitching post, got down and tied up his horse. "Nay, Emma. Please wait," he said when he saw Emma move as if to climb down. She waited while he skirted the buggy and reached up to lift her down. The warmth of her waist beneath his hands reminded him that she was someone he could care about. He released her quickly and stepped back in his attempt to put some emotional distance between them.

Without prompting, Emma entered the store with him following.

"Daniel," Bob Whittier said.

"Hallo," Daniel greeted warmly. "We've

come for ice cream." He looked at Emma. "Cup or cone?"

She glanced up at him shyly. "May I have a cone, please?"

He couldn't help but smile at her. "Two cones with chocolate chip mint ice cream."

"Coming right up," Bob said with a grin. He fixed their cones and handed each of them one with a couple of napkins.

"Thank you, Bob." Daniel paid the man. "Have a nice evening."

"Be careful to get home before the storm hits," the man warned. "The weather forecast is calling for a severe thunderstorm."

Daniel nodded. "We'll eat our ice cream and then be on our way." He and Emma went outside. He gestured toward a picnic table at the side of the building.

It was still bright. Fortunately, the earlier rain and cloud cover had disappeared. The sun shone on the horizon. The evening was cool, but Emma should be warm enough with her sweater. Of course, that could change once she started to eat her ice cream.

"Do you want a soda or a bottle of water?" Daniel asked, just thinking of it now.

"Nay, I'm fine. *Danki.*" She took a lick of her cone. "I haven't had ice cream in a long time."

Daniel gazed at her. "You haven't?"

She shook her head. "I appreciate this, Daniel. More than you'll ever know."

He frowned. Her voice was wistful, as if she were already thinking about the time she would leave. "We'll have to do this again," he said with conviction.

She merely smiled, looking sad.

They ate in silence for a time. Her sadness was a tangible thing. He could sense it and realized that she was in pain. "Emma," he began carefully, "what's wrong?"

"I'm fine," she said quickly. Too quickly.

He stayed silent. He wanted her to tell him about what Joseph had seen today.

Suddenly, she stiffened. "He told you," she said. "Joseph told you he thought I was stealing from Leah and Henry."

"*Ja*, he did," Daniel said, "and he also said that you said you weren't stealing but trying to pay for the garments Leah gave you."

She glanced at him with surprise. *"Ja."* There was only innocence in her beautiful brown eyes.

He smiled. "I know." He hadn't believed her capable of such deceit—not when he thought about it on the way over to the house. He felt as if he knew this woman inside and out, and he liked what he saw.

Her eyes warmed as she grinned at him. "*Danki*, Daniel."

He shrugged but held her gaze. He glanced down at her hands again. "Your cone is dripping."

She gasped and bent to lick it. And he laughed. Because he liked having her near. *She is an Englisher*, he reminded himself. *But she fits in so well*, a little voice inside argued. Only time would tell what the future held. He hoped it meant more of him spending time with her, but there was a big chance that she would leave and never return once she turned eighteen. Unless he could convince her that his Amish community and his family was where she belonged.

"We should get going," Daniel said.

Emma saw him eyeing the horizon. "Okay." She reached for his soiled napkins and threw them out.

He smiled at her as they walked back to his vehicle. He helped her up, then climbed onto the other side. The sky in the distance had darkened. It was far enough away that she thought they could both get home safely. Would the thunderstorm go on all night? If it did, she wouldn't be leaving this evening. She could go in the morning or tomorrow night.

She preferred to leave before the sun rose and not after sunset, with the long night of darkness making her feel unsafe.

Would she ever feel safe again once she left Missy and Arlin's home? She wished she could stay but knew she couldn't. Would Daniel be angry once he realized that she'd gone? She would try to explain everything to him in a note. She only hoped that he would understand and forgive her.

Emma was conscious of him sitting beside her, his competent hands on the reins. The night air had warmed considerably, which might have been due to the approaching storm. "Will you have enough time to get home safely after you drop me off?" she asked with concern.

Daniel met her gaze. "I'll have plenty of time."

She felt the tension of worry leave her body. *"Gut."* She thought of what she'd done in the store today. "Do you think Leah will notice that I put money in the register?"

"When they run a register accounting, they'll know."

She gasped and closed her eyes. She felt him shift beside her. She looked at him and was surprised to see him watching her through narrowed eyes. "How can I ever repay them if they refuse to take my money?" she said.

His expression softened. "Leah gave with her heart. She doesn't want to be repaid."

Warmth settled in her chest. "You are all so generous and giving." She sighed. "I've never met anyone like you…and your family." Emma saw his curiosity and averted her gaze. "When I was little, I had family who loved me, but that was long ago."

"Emma."

She hugged herself with her arms.

"Emma, look at me." She faced him, and he said, "You deserve more than you've had. You know that, don't you?"

Did she? "I guess so."

Daniel steered the carriage onto Arlin's property. "Know so," he stated firmly. He pulled close to the side door. He came around to help her down. "You look tired. I hope you sleep well."

She paused before going to the house. "*Danki* for a lovely evening, Daniel Lapp."

"You are more than *willkomm*, Emma Stoltzfus," he replied with a smile. "*Gut* night."

"*Gut* night." She turned away before he saw the tears in her eyes. Emma Stoltzfus, he'd called her, as if she already belonged to the family. She wouldn't see him again, and the knowledge pained her. She heard him leave, the sound of horse hooves and the contact of the metal buggy wheels against dirt and gravel.

"Farewell, Daniel Lapp," she breathed softly.

Emma wiped her eyes, drew herself up, pasted a smile on her face and entered the house, where she greeted Missy and Arlin and told them of the evening she'd spent with Daniel.

Three hours later, when she was in bed, the storm started as a low rumble of thunder. Emma had never been fond of thunderstorms. From an early age, she'd been frightened of the thunder. When her parents' deaths had occurred one rainy, stormy night, she'd become terrified instead of just scared. Every storm since then reminded her of the loss of her mother and father. She lay on her side with the covers pulled up over her chin, waiting for the full force of the storm to hit. When it did, she jumped every time there was a flash of lightning followed by a sharp crack of thunder. The rain fell in torrents, beating against the roof and obscuring the view outside. She pulled the covers up over her head but found little comfort. Were Missy and Arlin awake with all the noise? Emma didn't want to be alone. If they were up, she wanted to get up, too. Maybe then she'd find comfort in the safety of their kindness and caring.

She threw off the covers and got out of bed. Emma opened the door and peered into the hallway. There was no light in the room down the hall. Could they be downstairs? What of the animals? Would they be all right in the barn?

She went back into her room and grabbed her penlight. Switching it on, she left her bedroom and went downstairs. The penlight was slowly dying. *Please don't die yet.*

Emma made it to the bottom of the stairs. A light shone from the kitchen. Relieved, she rushed toward the room, halting when she saw Arlin and Missy at the kitchen table with steaming mugs. She was trembling when she entered.

"Can I join you?" she asked shakily.

"Emma." Missy took one look at her and hurried to her side. Slipping her arm around Emma's shoulders, she led her to a kitchen chair. "Sit, and I'll make you tea. Unless you want something cold?"

Emma hugged herself with her arms. "Tea is fine. *Danki.*"

"You don't like storms," Arlin said.

She shook her head. "I hate them."

"My Leah is—was—the same way. She's

been afraid since she was caught in a storm when she was only three."

Emma widened her eyes. "Leah afraid?"

"She was." He nodded. "Probably still is, but Henry has helped her tremendously. 'Tis funny how the love of a good man cures a lot of things."

Missy and Arlin exchanged loving looks. Emma thanked Missy when she placed a cup of tea on the table before her. She took a sip and realized that Missy had fixed her tea just the way she liked it. "I've always disliked thunderstorms," she admitted. "And it only got worse after my parents were killed in a car crash during a storm."

Missy took the seat beside Emma's. "I can't say I'm too comfortable with them myself. This one is particularly noisy. Neither one of us could sleep."

"*Ja*. I can't either."

"Tell us, Emma," Arlin urged with a small smile. "What do you think of our Daniel?"

Emma blushed. "He's nice."

"He's a fine young man."

She nodded.

"I think he likes you."

"I'm an Englisher," she reminded them. "He's polite because that is his nature."

"I don't think that's entirely true." Arlin took

a sip from his cup. "Didn't you like going for a ride with him?"

"I did," Emma murmured.

"You need to stop worrying about where you came from," Missy scolded kindly. "You're here with us now."

"*Ja*, I know, but—"

The woman shook her head to stop her. Emma sighed. If they ever found out who she was and what her family had done, she'd lose their kindness and respect. "Tell me about your daughters growing up," she asked, hoping to change the subject."

Arlin and Missy were more than willing to tell stories about each of their daughters. Emma was shocked to learn that Leah was their niece before they'd adopted her as their daughter. Missy's sister Christine had given birth to a baby girl but had been unable to care for her. Christine would come to visit her child—as an aunt. But then Leah's birth mother was killed in a car crash shortly after Leah's adoption was final.

Emma felt for the woman who had died. She'd been so young to have a baby, too young to die before she'd ever really lived.

Fortunately, Missy and Arlin loved Leah as if they'd given her life. The couple spoke lovingly of Charlie and Ellie and Nell and Meg.

Before Emma knew it, the storm had moved away, leaving the night quiet and peaceful. It was close to midnight when they went back to bed.

Missy stopped Emma at the top of the stairs. "'Tis late and you've barely slept. You should sleep in tomorrow morning. Don't worry about getting up to tend the animals."

"I don't mind."

"If you can sleep late, sleep, Emma," Arlin said with affection. "I'll handle the animals in the morning. You'll need to be well rested before you go to work."

Agreeing because she had no other choice as far as Missy and Arlin were concerned, Emma went to bed. She'd planned to leave tonight, but the storm—and the knowledge that Leah needed her to work—had her postponing her departure. What if she left and it stormed again? Where would she find shelter or sleep? How would she eat? The idea of sleeping in a barn again after enjoying a comfortable bed didn't sit well with her. She'd stay a little longer, and for now, she wouldn't think about being shunned or her departure.

As she lay in bed, Emma thought of her parents and how they hadn't regretted leaving their Amish church community. Now that she was living in Happiness as an Amish woman, she had so many questions for them.

She could stay until her eighteenth birthday. She liked the idea because it meant that she would see Daniel again until she had to leave. He said he'd buy her ice cream again. Would he take her before she left for good? She didn't care how she spend her time with Daniel, as long as she could enjoy more moments in his company. Moments she could store as precious memories before she had to go.

Chapter Eleven

Now that she'd decided to stay for the time being, Emma felt that her week was flying by quickly. Daniel took her to work each morning. Joseph picked her up each afternoon. The day after she'd put money in the register, Henry had done a register accounting. Joseph was in the store waiting for her when Henry had confronted her about what he'd found.

"The register tape doesn't match the cash in the drawer. There is too much money."

Joseph chuckled. "I know why," he said before Henry could accuse her of overcharging someone.

Emma glared at him. "Joseph."

"She put money in the register to pay for the garments Leah gave her."

Henry narrowed his gaze at her.

"I had no choice. You wouldn't take back

my pay," she said softly, his look making her avert her glance.

"Because you earned it, Emma," he replied quietly.

He sounded more resigned than angry. She met his gaze. "Please keep the money. 'Tis not much. *Please.* 'Tis important to me."

Leah's husband gazed at her steadily for a long moment, then sighed. She caught his reluctant nod. She grinned at him. *"Danki."*

When payday came around on Thursday, Henry paid her. "Don't even think about returning a single penny of it."

Emma smiled. *"Oll recht."*

Sunday was church service day. After helping Missy in the kitchen on Saturday, Emma rose while it was still dark and stared out the window as dawn was but a promise in the sky with barely enough light to see. She thought of how much her life had changed since coming to live with Missy and Arlin.

Emma dressed quickly, then went out to feed the animals. Sunday or not, taking care of them was a necessary task, thus allowed by the bishops. She did the work quickly, then returned inside to find Jeremiah asleep in his bed in the corner of the kitchen. As she shut the door behind her, the little dog woke and looked up at her. He stretched his black-and-white body before he came to her with a doggy grin and eyes that pleaded for attention.

Emma beamed at him. Jeremiah waited at the door for her to attach his leash. Then she opened the door and watched as the dog bounded outside, dragging her behind him. She laughed. "Jeremiah, stop, boy! Hold up. I'll get you where you want to go." She took him on a brisk walk and returned to the house. Missy and Arlin were in the kitchen when she came in. "What time do we need to leave for service?" she asked.

"Church is at nine. My sister and her husband are hosting today," Arlin told her.

Emma's belly began to flutter. "Daniel's parents?"

"Ja." Missy smiled at her. "Breakfast is ready—muffins and biscuits."

Her lips curved. "Sounds *wunderbor*." Emma sat in her usual place at the table across from Missy with Arlin beside her at the end. A cup of coffee steamed from its place above her plate. Emma saw it, then smiled at her Amish foster mother with gratitude.

"Eat," Missy urged with a small smile.

Emma grabbed a muffin, then reached for the butter that Arlin had passed to her. She took a bite, and the sweet taste hit her tongue, causing her to make a sound of appreciation.

When she realized that Missy and Arlin were staring at her, she blushed and carefully set the muffin on her plate. "I'm sorry. It's delicious."

Missy beamed while Arlin studied her with affection. "I'm glad you like it," Missy said. "'Tis *gut* that you enjoy your food, Emma. You were too thin when you first came to us."

Emma couldn't deny it. She hadn't been given enough to eat at the Turners'. She slowly picked up the muffin for another bite. The three of them enjoyed their breakfast in silence. When they were finished, Emma helped Missy put away the leftovers and threw out the paper plates they'd used.

"Why don't you get into your church clothes? I laid them out on your bed for you."

Emma stilled. "You got me new garments?"

"Just church clothes."

She blinked rapidly, close to tears. "*Danki*, Missy. I don't know what to say."

"You can say 'I'm getting ready for church,'" Missy said with good humor.

She grinned and headed upstairs.

The royal blue dress that lay on her bed looked brand-new, as if it had been specially made for her recently. Emma studied the garment and noted the tiny neat and even stitching. Missy's handiwork, she thought. She washed up, then changed into her new clothes.

Over the dress, she donned a white full-length apron. She undid her hair and brushed it, then rerolled and pinned it before covering it with the new white prayer *kapp* that had been on the bed next to the dress.

After putting on black stockings and shoes, Emma went back downstairs and entered the kitchen. She felt suddenly shy in her new garments. Arlin glanced at her as she came into the room, nodding his approval. "Wife," he called, and Missy turned from the counter, saw Emma and smiled.

"It fits you well."

Emma nodded.

Missy held up an iced tea pitcher. "Would you like some? There is still time for a cup before we need to leave."

"Is there any coffee left?" she asked.

"Ja." Missy poured her a fresh cup before Emma could do it herself. Emma sat.

"You took care of the animals this morning," Arlin said gruffly as he watched her pour some milk into her cup.

"Ja."

"And you took Jeremiah for a walk. For a little one, he has a lot of energy. 'Tis nice to have you pitch in with him."

Warmth filled her that Arlin was willing to share his precious pet with her. The three of them chatted to pass the time, which easily slipped by them. Missy glanced at the clock and stood. "We need to go if we don't want to be late for church service," she said.

Emma felt a sudden rush of nerves as she picked up a huge bowl of potato salad and carried it out to the buggy.

There would be a lot of people at the service. People she'd never met before. Daniel would be there along with his brothers, their wives, their children, his sister and his parents. And who knew what other members of the community. The thought of meeting so many new people scared her.

It was a short ride to the Samuel Lapp property. Arlin pulled his family buggy in at the end of a long line of parked carriages. Emma waited for him to tie up the horse, then she grabbed the potato salad they made for the midday meal and climbed out of the vehicle after Missy.

Her Amish foster mother carried a sheet cake. "There's Katie," she said, and started toward her sister-in-law. Emma immediately followed. She stopped when she caught sight of Daniel surrounded by three young women in the backyard. He was chatting and smiling as if he were enjoying their company.

Emma's gut clenched. Daniel was way too

handsome for her peace of mind. He was dressed like every other Amish man there, in a white shirt with black vest, black pants and a black felt wide-brimmed hat. She watched as one of the women said something to him and he laughed, drawing attention to the fact that he'd done very little laughing in her company. She liked the man, and she shouldn't. Their outing for ice cream had been the most fun she'd had in...forever. She looked away and continued toward the house.

"Emma?"

Emma turned and flushed when she saw Daniel's mother. "'Tis *gut* to see you again. We're glad you could come," Katie Lapp said. "Missy was telling me how much of a help you've been to her and Arlin."

"I like to help." She eyed Missy worriedly. "I'd like to do more."

Missy blinked. "Dear child, if you did anything more, there would be nothing at all for me to do." She placed a gentle hand on her shoulder. "You do more than enough. I wish you wouldn't work so hard."

Emma gazed at her with wide eyes. "I don't want you to have to work so hard." While she was here, she thought. For she'd be leaving soon. She sighed and looked away, toward the backyard—and Daniel.

Arlin joined them. He smiled at his sister. "Katie."

Katie grinned. "Always *gut* to see you, *bruder.*"

"Arlin!" Katie's husband Samuel waved him over to the group of men he was chatting with.

"They'll talk about the weather," Missy confided, "and who knows what else until 'tis time for service."

Emma managed a smile. She refused to look in Daniel's direction again, because seeing him with those other women hurt too much. "Shall I take the food inside?" she asked as she reached for the sheet cake with her other arm.

Katie smiled. "Of course." Emma nodded. "You can put the potato salad in the refrigerator if you can find room."

Balancing the large potato bowl and the sheet cake in a metal pan with lid, Emma climbed the porch steps, wondering how she would open the door with her hands full. She set the bowl on the arm of a porch chair and tugged open the door. With her hip holding it open, she leaned back for the potato salad. As she stretched to reach it, she saw a masculine hand pick it up for her. Emma looked back and drew a sharp breath. It was Daniel.

"May I carry this in for you?" he said with a twinkle in his eye.

She nodded, then entered the house.

"Straight through toward the back of the house," Daniel instructed from behind her. Heart thumping hard, she found the kitchen and set the cake on the counter. Conscious of Daniel behind her, she turned for the potato salad, but he had already placed it inside the refrigerator for her.

Soon he faced her. *"Danki,"* she murmured. Why was she comfortable with him one moment and uncomfortable the next?

Daniel nodded. "Nice dress," he said pleasantly.

She flushed with pleasure until she recalled him in the backyard with the other women.

Before she could formulate a response, the back door that led directly into the kitchen opened, and a young woman entered. Emma immediately recognized her as one of those women he'd been chatting with.

"Daniel! I wondered where you went," the woman said.

"Maryanne," he murmured.

She was blond, blue-eyed and beautiful. She made Emma feel like the ugly foster child in comparison. "Who is this?" Maryanne said with a long look at Emma.

"This is Emma. She is a cousin from my aunt's side of the family." His expression softened as he met Emma's gaze. "Emma, meet Maryanne Troyer. Her family moved into our church district a few months ago."

Emma shifted uncomfortably under the woman's blue gaze. "'Tis nice to meet you," she murmured.

"Same here," the woman said without warmth.

Something flashed in Daniel's expression. Emma couldn't read his thoughts, but she suddenly felt as if she were intruding. She needed to get away. "Excuse me. Missy is waiting," she said, and headed toward the back door.

"I'll walk you out," Daniel piped up, shocking her.

Emma caught a glimpse of something dark flash in the woman's blue gaze. "Daniel," she called out as he followed Emma. "You'll be attending the singing this evening, *ja*?"

"I might be," he said. "But that will depend on Emma." Then to her surprise, he reached for Emma's hand and tugged her to exit the house, only releasing her to grab the door and hold it open for her.

Emma rushed ahead of him toward Missy, who was still talking with Katie.

"Emma," Daniel said, halting her, prompting her to face him. "Don't let her upset you. She's immature for her age."

"*Danki*, Daniel." Emma noticed that Katie and Missy were moving toward the barn. She hurried to join them for church service.

Missy turned as Emma caught up with her. "Just in time."

She nodded, following Missy and Katie into the barn. To her surprise, Daniel caught up to her and entered the barn alongside her.

The pulpit was surrounded on three sides by benches. Daniel parted ways with her to take a seat in the left section where men were already seated. Missy waved for her to follow toward the right where women and their children sat. Emma sat next to Missy and watched as others quietly filed in. A man moved to the pulpit and waited for everyone to enter and be seated. Women and children filled the middle and far side while the men sat with their older sons in the section where Daniel had taken a seat.

Once all church members were seated, the preacher started to speak. Emma listened carefully and watched the others in the room who looked intent, engaged. Everyone stood and began to sing, an odd chanting sound without

musical instruments. The song—a hymn—
spiked a childhood memory. The way the
hymn was sung might be different, but she remembered the words as clearly as if she'd sung
them yesterday. Her lips began to move as she
joined in. When the hymn ended, she listened
closely to the preacher and felt a strong sense
of God in the room. Just like when she'd been
to service with her *mam* and *grossmamma*.
Memories of the past flooded her. Fighting
tears, she closed her eyes and offered up a silent prayer for everything she'd lost and everything she wished for. A life with a family like
the Stoltzfuses and the Lapps. A life filled with
love and caring without the terror and threat
of the Turners, her foster family.

The service continued with another hymn
and the deacon adding a few words of wisdom
before church finally ended at midday. Emma
rose and followed Missy outside. The day had
begun with cool temperatures but had warmed
up considerably. She looked for Daniel, but
didn't see him.

Missy touched her arm, drawing her attention. "Follow me. We need to put the food out."

She nodded and trailed after her toward the
house. As she crossed the yard, she saw Daniel
standing alone, leaning against a buggy. Their
eyes met, and Emma's cheeks grew warm. She

forced her attention on being part of the community and found she liked the feeling of belonging. It brought back memories of her time in Indiana and the love of her family.

Emma helped the other women put out all the food, then sat with the Stoltzfuses and their daughters and their families at one of the makeshift tables that the men had set up in the yard. A large plate of food lay before her on the table, but she wasn't hungry. Her stomach churned as she attempted to eat. Her thoughts centered on Daniel. She tried not to stare in his direction, but he continually drew her attention.

"Are you *oll recht*?" Leah smiled as she sat down next to her.

Emma nodded. "I'm fine. How are you feeling?"

"Big."

She grinned. "Have you been getting enough rest?"

Leah chuckled. "I have, thanks to you."

"Leah, I don't know how to—"

"Emma, don't say it," Leah warned with a frown.

Dread filled her stomach. "What?"

"Don't tell me how grateful you are and how you need to repay me."

She averted her gaze. "But I do."

"From what Henry told me, you already did. You put money in the cash register. Over a hundred dollars!"

"You gave me a job, clothes and a home with your parents." Emma would leave another hundred dollars for Missy and Arlin when she left. She'd be fine now that she'd earned a second week's pay. With nearly three hundred dollars, she'd be able to travel farther than if she'd left on Monday when originally planned.

Leah regarded her with a soft expression. "You deserve everything, and I'll keep telling you that until you believe it."

"Anyone for dessert?" Leah's sister Charlie said as she approached.

Leah and Emma grinned. "We are," they both said together.

She would enjoy her time here, know that God had blessed her with these people, and she would thank Him every day while here and after she'd gone.

"I want the chocolate cake," Emma said.

"Me, too," Leah declared. "But why don't we try a little of everything?"

Emma smiled. "Sounds *gut* to me." She stood and followed Leah to the dessert table, catching Daniel's eye as she did. Her heart stopped beating as he continued to watch her, his expression unreadable, until she forced herself to move on and focus on enjoying dessert with Leah and the Stoltzfus family.

A short while later, with a dessert plate on the table before her, she rose to pour herself an iced tea. Standing at the drink table, she sensed Daniel beside her.

"Emma," he said warmly. "Would you like to take a ride after lunch? I'll ask Joseph and Hannah to come with us," he added, as if she needed convincing.

She looked up into his brown eyes, and she couldn't say no. "*Ja*, I'd like that."

His smile made her heart beat faster. "I'll tell Joseph and Hannah. Let me know when you're done with dessert."

Emma nodded, watching as he headed to his family table where he spoke briefly with his brother and sister. She saw both smile as they gazed in her direction.

Anticipation ran wild as she enjoyed her dessert. When she was done, she put her paper plate and plasticware in the trash, then turned to look for Daniel. He was already approaching her. She smiled at him as he reached her.

"Ready to go?"

"*Ja*, just let me tell Missy and Arlin."

"Joseph is telling them now."

Surprised, Emma saw that Joseph and Hannah were talking with their aunt and uncle. "What is he saying to them?"

A small smile of amusement played about his lips. "Who knows? As long as we get to go, I don't care what they tell them."

Emma raised her eyebrows. "Daniel…"

"I'm teasing, Emma. They're simply telling them we're going for a ride to check out locations."

"Locations?" she asked.

"I'm looking for a place to open a harness shop."

"I remember that," she said.

"I should be able to open it by next month at the latest."

After I'm gone, Emma thought. She would have liked to see his business, watch him at work. He would be talented and dedicated, intent on providing excellent service to his customers.

"Is that why we're going for a ride?"

"I want to take you on a ride because I like spending time with you," he admitted.

Her breath caught. "I don't know what to say."

"Tell me you won't change your mind."

"I won't."

"We'll take the open wagon," Daniel said

to Joseph as his brother and sister reached their sides.

"Sounds *gut* to me."

"You'll ride in the back with Hannah," Daniel whispered to his brother, but Emma heard him.

Daniel wanted her to ride in the front seat with him. She felt lighthearted and happy. It was if God were smiling down on her and granting her secret wish. That Daniel would like her and want to be close to her. But no matter what happened in the future, she felt forever changed by her time here.

Chapter Twelve

The afternoon started out pleasantly. Emma sat in Daniel's open carriage and took in the scenery. The air was fresh and she took a deep breath…detecting a pleasant masculine scent that was Daniel's.

Joseph and Hannah sat behind them. Daniel's siblings teased each other mercilessly and made amusing comments about various members of their family. Joseph teased Daniel for a long while about making Emma sit up front with him.

"Where are we going, *bruder*?" Hannah asked after he turned onto a country lane with vast open farmland on both sides of the road.

"No place special. Just taking a drive to show Emma the area," he said.

Emma met his gaze. "Is there someplace in particular you want me to see?"

He grinned at her. "Nay, but if I see something interesting, we'll stop and take a look."

Daniel steered the horse through several turns that took them onto a number of country roads. They passed an ice cream shop in the middle of nowhere. "They make great ice cream here," he told her. "We'll come back when the place is open. 'Tis run by members of our community, and therefore it's closed on Sundays."

Emma loved that Daniel had suggested another outing together. If things continued to go well, she'd be able to enjoy going for ice cream with him. If not…she didn't want to think about her situation and how she could be long gone before she ever had a chance to drive back for ice cream.

Thoughts of Bryce Turner gave her chills, and she rubbed her arms.

"Cold?" Daniel asked after a glance in her direction.

"I'm fine." His concern made her feel good. She was safe with Daniel. Bryce would never search for her in an Amish community. She was sure of it.

Daniel drove through a few turns, then headed back toward the main road. Before they reached it, Emma saw it—a white house set back from the country lane about a hundred feet or more. Next to it was a small barn and beyond that a smaller outbuilding. The house was plain enough for her to believe that it belonged to an Amish family. There was a for-sale sign in the front yard.

Without thinking, Emma instinctively put her hand on Daniel's arm. "Daniel..."

"I see it," he breathed. He pulled over to the side of the road. The sign had a phone number and said the house was for sale by the owner. "Joseph, would you come up front and take care of the horse?"

Daniel climbed down from the vehicle. "Emma?" He reached up a hand, and she allowed him to lift her down. Together they both walked down the fine gravel driveway toward the house.

"Do you think anyone is home?"

He stared at the house. "I don't think anyone is living here at present."

Emma nodded. She accompanied him to the house. They went to the front door, and he knocked. After waiting a few moments, Daniel knocked again. "You're right. Looks like no one is here."

Without saying anything, they went to a window and looked in. There was no furniture. The vinyl floors looked as if they had been installed recently. They walked around to the back of the house and saw a kitchen with a refrigerator and stove as well as oak cabinets. "It looks nice," Emma murmured.

"Ja," Daniel said quietly. Emma could sense his excitement. As if he liked what he saw and was considering buying it. Emma envisioned Daniel living here with a wife—some other woman—and felt a sadness wash over her. But she couldn't worry about that. She was here with Daniel right now, and she was glad that he allowed her to share this with him.

"Shall we look at the barn and outbuilding?" Emma asked.

"Gut idea." But Daniel was already moving in that direction. He went to the barn first and opened the door. The inside was empty, the stalls clean. So far everything was in move-in condition. Then he led her to the small building in the backyard. It was a ten-by-ten building with a window. The door opened easily, and whatever he saw inside made him gasp. "Perfect," he said. "This place is perfect."

Emma knew then that Daniel wanted this place—and badly. She said a silent prayer that he would be able to afford it, that no one jumped in to purchase it out from under him before he had his chance to make an offer.

He shut the door. "We should go," he said quietly. His expression was thoughtful, worried. At that moment, Emma wanted to give him all the money she had—just under three hundred dollars. If it helped him realize his dream, she'd be fine with giving it all away. She'd figure out a way to get by once she left Happiness. She'd done it before, and she could do it again.

The ride home with Daniel back at the reins was quieter than when they'd started out.

"Nice place, Daniel," Joseph said. "Going to buy it?"

"If I can, *ja*," Daniel muttered, his grip tight on the leathers.

Emma felt the urge to cover his hand with hers. "You'll find a way," she murmured, believing it to be true.

He shot her a surprised look. Staring at her a moment, his face erupted into a genuine smile. "*Danki*, Emma."

She frowned. "For what?"

"For believing in me."

She blushed and looked away. He was more than competent in anything he did. Why did he question it? Unlike her, who couldn't decide what to do. The best thing she'd ever done was come back to Happiness to see Leah. She sighed. Her temporary place with the Stoltzfuses was nothing she could take credit for. It was because of Leah and Henry and everyone else.

* * *

Daniel heard Emma sigh. "What's wrong?"

She smiled at him reassuringly. "Nothing to worry about." She paused. "My birthday is in three weeks."

"And you'll be eighteen," he said gruffly. The thought of her leaving bothered him, although he'd always known that the day would come. "It's too bad you couldn't stay here…" he murmured.

He felt her tense and sensed her gaze on him. "Forever? Daniel…"

"I know. You can't stay." *You don't want to stay*, he thought bitterly.

"I don't belong here," she whispered.

Daniel looked in her eyes, saw the sorrow in them, the tears. Something jolted inside him. "Emma—"

"Hey, look!" his sister exclaimed, pointing toward a vehicle parked on the side of the road close to the dirt entrance to his family's property.

"That's David Fisher," Joseph said with surprise.

Hannah started to stand up to better see. "Do you think he's come to ask forgiveness?"

"Could be," Daniel said, but he doubted it. The man was seated in his buggy, and he hadn't made a move to get out. No doubt he missed his family members who were in his parents' house.

Daniel turned on his left blinker and turned into the lot. "Don't look at him. Don't make eye contact," he told Emma and his siblings. "I hate this, but 'tis not allowed since he was shunned."

Emma hadn't said a word, but he could feel her withdraw from him, her shoulders so tense that he wanted to reach out and rub them for her. Which, of course, he would never do, as it wasn't proper unless they were husband and wife. Daniel's jaw tightened. Which they'd never be, as she would be leaving them—*him*—in three weeks. Suddenly, the excitement of finding the perfect place for his business and new home disappeared. But he would work for it anyway. Whether Emma stayed or not, he would start his harness shop business, and eventually wed and start a family.

Emma didn't wait for his help getting out of the carriage. He watched her stride toward his aunt and uncle and their family, watched her speak to Leah, who frowned and stood up to follow Emma, who moved away from the others.

What was she telling them? Was she reminding them that her birthday was just around the corner and she'd be leaving soon? Was she telling them about David Fisher, the shunned man who had parked his buggy in the street in front of the house?

Emma left Leah and went to the beverage table. He watched her pour two cups of tea. To his shock, she headed in his direction. "I thought you might be thirsty," she said softly. She held out a cup to him.

He held her gaze, begging to know her thoughts, as he nodded and took the cup from her. He smiled his thanks.

"I had a nice time today, Daniel," she began carefully, and he sensed a "but" coming. "I hope you get the house and the property. It's perfect for your business and your home. I'll be thinking of you living there someday, happy with a wife." She stopped. "And children."

"Emma, we still have time to spend together."

She shook her head. "Do you think that's wise? Knowing that I'll have to leave?"

"I don't care if 'tis wise. I want to see you and take you for ice cream again. We can go to that ice cream shop we saw today, or we can go back to Whittier's." He took a sip from his cup. It was all he could do to keep his hands steady as he lowered his drink. "Think about it, Emma."

She nodded. "I will."

And he could only hope and pray that God would allow him to find a way to keep them together, because Englisher or not, he wanted Emma in his life—as he was realizing more and more that she was already in his heart.

She remained by his side for the next hour until Missy and Arlin decided it was time to go home. She'd been overly quiet since their conversation about ice cream and spending more time together.

"I'll see you in the morning, Emma," he said as he walked her toward Arlin's carriage.

Emma frowned as she looked up at him. "In the morning?"

"To take you to work? At the Yoders' store," he gently reminded her.

"Ah, *ja.* Sorry."

"Emma, are you *oll recht*?"

"I'm fine." Her smile—which didn't quite reach her eyes—didn't reassure him. "I'll see you tomorrow."

As he watched her leave with his aunt and uncle, he felt an ache inside his chest. And a sense of foreboding he didn't understand.

Daniel joined his parents, who were talking with Bishop John. David Fisher was a relative of the bishop's, and John was unhappy with the man. "You saw the buggy parked out front, Bishop?" he asked as he came close.

The bishop nodded. "I'd hoped that he would come in, but if he expects us to accept what he's done when he shows no repentance, it's not going to happen."

"Would you like me to approach him?" his father asked.

"Nay, he knows the rules. We are not to talk with him, look at him or do business with him. If he wants to enjoy the delights of the English world, he should have thought of that before he joined the church."

Daniel couldn't imagine being ostracized by his family. He loved and needed them too much to ever give them up. Plus, he couldn't think of any reason he'd ever go against the Ordnung. He excused himself with a nod toward the bishop and his parents.

Daniel sought out his cousin Leah, who was there with her husband Henry.

Leah saw him heading her way. She left her sisters and family to meet him halfway. "You look as if you have something on your mind."

Daniel nodded. "May I talk with you?"

"Ja." She settled one hand on her protruding stomach while the other one waved him away from anyone who remained.

When they were alone on the side of his father's barn, Daniel met her gaze. "I like Emma."

Leah laughed. "No kidding."

His expression grew serious, concerned. "She'll be eighteen soon, and then she'll be leaving."

"I know," his cousin murmured with sympathy.

"Tell me what they did to her. Her foster parents."

"Her foster father and brother," Leah said.

Daniel felt his jaw tighten with tension. "Tell me."

"That day when you brought her to me? She had bruises on her arms. I made her show me, but I think she hid the worst of them."

"They mistreated her?"

"*Ja*, emotionally and physically."

"She needs to stay with us," he stated firmly. "With me."

"Emma may be hard to convince, but if anyone can, 'tis you." Leah eyed him with a small smile. "She cares for you."

Emotion rushed through him, and he closed his eyes. "I hope so."

"Have patience with her, Daniel," she said. "Love is worth it. I almost gave that up with Henry because I was afraid. Don't let her be afraid, Daniel. She needs you, and you need her."

Daniel smiled as determination rose up in him to give him more than hope. It gave him purpose. He wanted that house and land more than anything. Emma might be English, but he believed she'd be happy within the Amish community. He'd seen her grow from an unhappy runaway foster child to a warm, loving and hardworking young woman.

"I'll convince her," he said, and at that moment he believed it.

It was time. After a wonderful evening at home with Arlin and Missy, Emma went upstairs to bed—and to plan. While she wanted to give Daniel all of her money, she knew it wouldn't make sense for her to do so. She'd need every cent for a safe place to stay until she turned eighteen and got another job. She would miss Missy and Arlin. The thought of leaving them hurt terribly. But it was the knowledge that she wouldn't see Daniel again that broke her heart. She'd never be the same after her time here. Knowing that she'd had the love of these people, even for a short time, would sustain her through the long lonely days and nights ahead of her.

She lay in her bed, still dressed, listening as Missy and Arlin ascended the stairs and retired to their room at the end of the hall. Her heart thumped wildly in her chest. Her stomach burned, and her hands were clammy. She was scared. She wrote a note and placed it on the dresser. After another hour or so, when she was sure Missy and Arlin were asleep, she rose, took her money and put most of it in her shoes. Fortunately, the sky was clear, the stars twinkling brightly against an inky backdrop. There would be no rain tonight, no thunderstorms to terrify her during her journey.

She pulled on her sweater and buttoned it all the way up. She glanced at her Amish garments. Traveling in them wouldn't be ideal, but it was all she had now. She hadn't seen her English clothes since she left them with Leah. If she found a thrift store, she could buy some clothes. She'd draw less attention to herself if she blended better in the English world.

She left a hundred dollars on the bed, covering it with the note. She hoped Missy and Arlin would understand, and that Daniel would forgive her.

Her heart was breaking as she grabbed the new flashlight that Missy had given her recently and descended the stairs. Jeremiah was in the kitchen, curled up in his bed. She figured it was best to leave him there when she went up earlier, but now she wondered if it wouldn't have been better to lock him in her room.

The little dog had received a lot of attention from her when they'd returned home. He was obviously tired, and her crossing the kitchen to the side door didn't wake him. Sending up a silent prayer of thanks to the Lord, Emma opened up the side door, turned the lock on the inside, then pulled the door quietly shut behind her. She headed into the night with her destination unknown. *Daniel.* What she wouldn't give to see him one more time. If she did, she knew her resolve would weaken, and she'd stay. And she would risk losing him when he learned the truth. *It's better this way.*

She was blinded by her tears as she left the property and headed away from Happiness, away from the city of Lancaster where the threat of discovery still remained. She would walk until she found a hotel that she could afford, even if it was just for one night. She had two hundred and sixty-eight dollars after leaving the money for Missy and Arlin. Poor payment for a lifetime of warm and happy memories, she thought. They deserved so much more from her.

The sound of a car behind her made her take cover in the bushes in a neighbor's front yard. When the vehicle roared passed, she walked along the side of the road again, quickening her steps. She needed to get somewhere fast so she could feel safe again.

If she ever would feel safe again.

* * *

Daniel steered his buggy toward Missy and Arlin's house. He was eager to see Emma. He'd been awake most of the night thinking of her, trying to figure out a way to convince her that she should stay in Happiness. And wed him when she was older and ready for marriage. He pulled into his uncle's yard and parked. It was early, but he knew Arlin and Missy would be up. Emma, too.

He tied up his horse and ran to the side door. He tapped on the wood and smiled when as expected his aunt opened it with a grin. "Daniel, come in."

"Mornin', *Endie* Missy." He saw his uncle at the table. "*Onkel* Arlin."

His uncle nodded. "If you're looking for Emma, I'd check the barn. I haven't seen her this morning, but that's where she always is first thing."

Daniel grinned, then nearly ran toward the barn. He burst inside. "Emma!"

No one answered. "Emma! 'Tis me. Daniel. I'd like to talk with you." When she didn't answer, he checked every inch of the structure, then hurried back to the house to see if she'd come down for breakfast. "She's not in the barn," he said as he entered.

"She was tired last night," Missy said.

"Maybe she slept late." She set a mug of coffee for him on the table. "Sit. I'll go up and check on her."

Daniel sat down to drink his coffee. He heard thundering on the stairs before Missy appeared, her face distraught, a handful of twenty-dollars bills in one hand and a note in the other.

"She's gone," she cried. "Emma left us. She's gone!"

Arlin stood and took the note from her. Daniel rose, his stomach clenching as he thought of the woman he loved and where she could have possibly gone. His uncle's features changed as he read Emma's note. When he was done, he silently handed Daniel the note and sat down, his face ashen.

Dear ones,
You will never know just how much your
kindness has meant to me. I have felt
truly happy here, and if things in my life
were different, I would have stayed. But
I'm trouble. Bryce Turner will no doubt
be searching for me. I saw something I
shouldn't have seen before I ran away.
He is not a gut man. Bryce is evil, and so
is his son. I love you and will miss you.
Please pray for me, although truth be told

*I don't deserve your attention or your
prayers. Please thank Leah and Henry
for me. Without Leah, I would not have
enjoyed even a few moments of feeling
safe and loved. Tell them I'm sorry.*

There was a spot on the page that looked as
if it had been marked by a tear. Daniel felt his
throat tighten.

*Please tell Daniel that I will miss him.
He is* gut *and kind, and I will never forget him. He needs to buy that house and
property we looked at. It is right for
him, and in the future, as I look back at
my time with him—with all of you—I'll
think of him happy with his business on
the property, and a wife with children in
that house. I'm so sorry for all the trouble
I've caused. Know in my heart that I'll always look upon you as family. You were
there for me when no one else cared.
Love, Emma.*

Daniel looked at his aunt and uncle. They
appeared as destroyed by the note as he was.
"I have to look for her."

"Where?" Arlin said.

"Anywhere. Everywhere," Daniel said. "And

while I'd love to ask everyone to search for her, I believe if she sees any of us, she'll bolt again. I need to do this on my own. If I can't find her, I'll let you know." He drew in a sharp breath. "I don't want to involve the police. Emma is terrified of them. She's afraid she'll be sent back to her foster family, and we can't allow them to do that to her."

Arlin nodded. "Whatever you think is best."

"How can I help?" Missy said hoarsely, her eyes filled with tears.

The sight of their tears brought home how much the young runaway Englisher had worked her way into their hearts. *Especially mine.*

He chose Emma over his job at the construction company. There was no question in his mind that he needed to find her. He stopped by Whittier's Store first to call his foreman from Bob's phone to explain that he wouldn't be able to make it in to work today. The man was pleasant enough, although Daniel knew he wouldn't be happy if he called out for more than two days straight. But he would if he had to. He could get the property, but without Emma nothing would be the same. And if he didn't find her today? He would keep searching for her—and he would make an offer for the house and have it ready for when he eventually found her.

As he steered his buggy to the edge of the parking lot at Whittier's, Daniel thought about where to look first. How much money did she have? She probably had made one hundred eighty dollars the first week and two hundred eighty-eight dollars her second week at the Yoders'. She'd put a hundred from her first week into the register. Then left Missy and Arlin a hundred dollars on the bed. After two weeks of work, that would leave almost three hundred dollars that she took with her.

He drew the horse to a halt and thought hard. Where would she go? She had enough money for a hotel room. At least for one night, he thought, maybe more. Daniel remembered how she didn't want to enter the city of Lancaster. *She'll go in the opposite direction.*

He flicked the leathers and turned away in the direction he thought she'd head. "Emma, where did you go?"

Chapter Thirteen

Emma walked through the night without incident. Every time she heard a car or truck, she hid so no one would see her. She was cold, but she'd be fine as soon as she found a room for the night she could afford. She paused to rest a moment and realized she'd been foolish not to bring food with her. But she'd never steal from Missy and Arlin.

Emma walked until she reached a small hotel that promised a free breakfast and a room for sixty-eight dollars a night. She hadn't gone far, but it didn't matter. She was ready to get out of the night air. The hotel belonged to a familiar chain, and she figured she'd be safe there. The light was on in the front office. She entered with her small bag of belongings and approached the reservation desk. Wearing her Amish garments, she didn't look as bad as when she'd first arrived in Happiness in her threadbare English clothes. And she had money.

"I'd like a room for one night, please," she told the night manager.

The woman looked at her. "Credit card?"

"Nay." Emma shook her head. "But I have cash."

"All right. It's your lucky day. You have a choice—first or second floor?"

"Second floor, please."

"That'll be seventy dollars," the woman said.

Emma handed over the money, and the manager handed her a room key. "Breakfast is in a room off the lobby between six and nine thirty."

Emma nodded, then with key in hand, she headed toward the elevator. She found her room on the second floor and let herself in. The room was clean and had recently been scrubbed, the scent of cleaning products still in the air. A virtual paradise to someone who thought she'd have to stay in a dirty hotel somewhere. And with the added benefit of breakfast. She glanced at the alarm clock on the night table and saw that it was nearly eleven. She put her things inside a dresser drawer and hid her money in a sock, which she shoved between the mattress and bedspring. She'd put out a do-not-disturb sign whenever she left the room until she checked out. She just needed a place to rest and recharge and figure out what to do next. She set the alarm for 6:00 a.m., hoping that there would be no one at breakfast at such an early hour. Then Emma slipped beneath the covers and closed her eyes. All she could think about was Daniel and how upset he'd be once he learned she'd left.

If she didn't have the threat of Bryce Turner—or if she hadn't been shunned by her former Amish community along with her parents—she might have found a way to stay. Because she'd loved it there. But she had to keep focused on the future. Maybe tomorrow after she'd eaten and returned to her room, she could make some plans past this one night. She wouldn't get far on the money she had. Maybe she could find a job in a small town. She knew how to work a cash register. And she could wait tables. Except she was underage, and she didn't have anything to prove how old she was.

She slept until her alarm went off, then she got up, got dressed and went downstairs for breakfast. As she hoped and prayed for, there were no other diners at that early hour. Emma nodded to the night manager who was still on duty, then proceeded to fill up a plate. There were trays of eggs and sausages. And there was a waffle iron with a pitcher of batter if she wanted waffles. She chose eggs, sausage, a biscuit and an apple. She filled a cup with hot water and grabbed a tea bag, then headed upstairs to eat in her room.

As she ate breakfast, she thought of Daniel and the people she'd left behind. *Why did I leave? I had people who cared for me.* A safe place to stay until her birthday. She was doubting herself, wondering if she'd made a mistake leaving Happiness. After finishing her food, she made another cup of tea using the room's electric coffeepot. As she sipped her tea, she thought of Missy and their tea times together. She closed her eyes as she fought back tears. She'd let down everyone—Leah and Henry. Missy and Arlin. Daniel and the Lapps.

Could she go back? Apologize and ask for another chance? Would they welcome her with open arms or send her away?

"What do I have to lose?" she whispered aloud. She finished her tea, packed her few belongings and stowed her money in her shoes. She hadn't come that far. Maybe she could return before they missed her.

She went downstairs, handed in the room key and left. Emma realized that she needed to get back to Happiness. She would ask for another chance and hope they would understand that she was confused.

Emma exited the hotel and headed back the way she'd come. While she walked, she prayed and pleaded for another chance and hoped that God would lead the way back home.

Daniel drove east on Route 340, away from Bird in Hand toward Intercourse, where he pulled into the parking lot near a coffee shop. He went inside to order a cup of coffee and some pastries to share with Emma when he found her. A police officer was at the counter, waiting for his order. Daniel thought nothing of it until he saw the officer show a photo to the girl behind the counter.

"Have you seen this teenager?" the officer asked.

The girl shook her head. "I'm afraid not."

Daniel stepped up and gave his order to the girl, then turned to the officer. "You're looking for someone?" he asked casually.

The officer met his gaze. "Yes. A teen runaway from Maryland." He shoved the photo in Daniel's direction. "Her foster family is eager to get her back."

Daniel took the photo and studied it with a calm gaze while his heart beat faster and his stomach started to burn. It was Emma. Dressed in English clothes. He handed the photo back. "Can't help you." He paused. "What's her name? In case I see her," he added. He expected to hear Jessica Morgan and was stunned at the name the officer gave.

"Emma Beiler."

"Why did she run away?" Daniel asked.

The officer frowned. "That's the thing. I found her the last time she ran away. Running away a second time makes me wonder if everything was as it should have been at her foster home." He tucked the photo in his shirt pocket. "I was hoping to find her and talk with her. Find out how things really were for her there."

Daniel received his order and followed the officer outside. "What should I do if I see her?"

The officer hesitated. "Get in touch with me." He handed Daniel a business card with a phone number and the address of his police station.

"I'll do that." Daniel gave him a nod. "Have a nice day, Officer." He untied his horse and debated which way to go next. He doubted she would continue east. Maybe south? There were a lot of hotels and motels along Lincoln Highway. Would she have looked for a cheap place to spend the night?

Emma Beiler. Her name was Emma Beiler.

He didn't know if he should be angry or not. She could have lied about her identity because she feared getting caught.

Would she check into a hotel under her own name? Use Jess Morgan or a different alias?

Daniel steered his buggy south. It was still early. Looking for her was like searching for a needle in a haystack. He sighed. He could head back in case she decided to return on her own, although he doubted she would. Fear for her safety rose within him. He needed to find her and convince her to return. Why did she leave? What triggered her sudden desire to go? Because he'd told her he enjoyed spending time with her?

He continued to search for her, driving south and then heading north again. Then suddenly he saw her. An Amish girl walking along the road. There was something about the set of her shoulders, the way she moved, that he instantly recognized her. He pulled up beside her.

She stopped walking and faced him. "Daniel?"

He stared at her. "Get in, Emma."

"I was on my way home," she told him.

He felt something inside him soften, but he needed answers, not only for himself but for Missy and Arlin and Leah and Henry.

Emma didn't move. "Please, Emma," he said. "Get in and I'll take you home."

She blinked rapidly but raised her chin. Then she crossed the road and climbed into his vehicle.

"Where did you spend the night?" he asked.

She released a sharp breath. "In a hotel. It came with free breakfast."

"What made you decide to return?"

"Because I realized that I was letting everyone down—Leah and Henry. Missy and Arlin." She sniffed. "You."

"I'm just glad you're *oll recht*," he said huskily.

"You were looking for me?"

"*Ja*. Ever since I went to the house to take you to work and discovered that you'd left." He ran his gaze over her, hoping to read her thoughts. "Why did you leave, Emma?"

"Because I don't deserve to stay."

"Yet you were coming back to us."

"*Ja*. Because I couldn't stay away."

He was more than a little upset with her. But could she blame him? She'd left without a word—just a note. It must have hurt Missy and Arlin terribly to find it. To know that she'd left them after they'd given her a home, love…

Emma took surreptitious glances at the man

sitting beside her. Would Missy and Arlin be angry as well? She wondered what time it was. Did Leah and Henry know that she'd left, abandoned them in their time of need? She closed her eyes.

The Arlin Stoltzfus house loomed ahead. Daniel turned onto the property, and Emma's heart started to hammer. She felt sick to her stomach when she saw that there was another buggy on the property. Leah and Henry's?

Daniel pulled his vehicle behind theirs. He jumped down, tied up his horse, but didn't come around to help Emma out. He was angry with her, she thought.

Expecting worse inside, Emma headed toward the house, knocked on the side door and waited. The door opened, and Missy stood there as if in shock. Then with a cry, she opened the door and pulled Emma inside. The woman hugged her. Arlin sat at the kitchen table, looking haggard. Henry and Leah had taken the chairs across from him. They took one look at her, then as one, they stood. "You're back," Leah said.

She nodded.

"Where did Daniel find you?" Henry asked.

"On the road. I was on my way back here. I…" Tears filled her eyes. "I shouldn't have left." She turned away. "I'm sorry," she whispered brokenly.

Daniel had come in behind her. Emma was aware that everyone was staring at her.

"When did you leave?" Missy asked.

Emma blushed. "Last night, after you were asleep."

"Where did you spend the night?" Leah asked.

"At a hotel. I… I didn't want to sleep in a barn." Her head was throbbing, and she lifted a hand to rub her temple.

Missy nodded. Arlin hadn't said a word. Emma knew that she had hurt him. She shouldn't have left but since she did, maybe she should have stayed away.

"I know I shouldn't have left, but I think 'tis for the best. You don't need me here."

Arlin stood abruptly. "Nay, you will not leave, *dochter*. You will go upstairs and think about what you did and how your disappearance affected the rest of us."

Emma gaped at him. Joy hit her hard when she realized he'd called her his daughter. "*Ja*, Arlin."

When she left the kitchen, it was silent. No one said a word. Clutching her small bag, she went up to her bedroom. She went inside, set down her bag, then lay on the bed, staring at the ceiling. She wouldn't hurt them by leaving again. Not until she turned eighteen and they expected it from her. She felt emotionally overwrought and exhausted. Emma closed her eyes and slept.

"The police are searching for her," Daniel said.

Missy and Arlin exchanged concerned glances.

"You spoke with an officer?" Leah asked.

"*Ja*. I stopped in a coffee shop for something to drink. The officer was showing her photo to the girl behind the counter."

"What did he say?"

Daniel pulled out a seat and sat at the table with the rest of them. "That she's a runaway foster child from Maryland." He rubbed the back of his neck wearily. "The officer did express concern that despite her foster father's eagerness to get her back, things might not be what the man is claiming. That she is his daughter in every way except by birth."

"*Ja*, we know the truth. It was a terrible situation for her," Leah said.

"There is something else you should know."

"What is it?" Missy asked. Arlin leaned forward with his arms on the tabletop.

"The girl lied to us about her identity. Her real name is not Jess Morgan. 'Tis Emma Beiler."

Leah smiled, seemingly unconcerned. "No wonder she said she could easily answer to Emma. The name was my idea."

Daniel hesitated. He was hurt by the way Emma had left and the fact that she'd lied to all of them. He had confessed that he liked to spend time with her—and she'd run away. "Are you going to keep her at the store?"

"*Ja*, she's a *gut* worker," Leah said.

Daniel glanced at Henry.

"I don't have any problem with it. She's proven trustworthy at work."

Something shifted inside him. "Why did she leave?" He hoped that they had an answer and it wasn't the same one he'd come up with on his own. "Her birthday is in less than three weeks."

"I know." Missy appeared concerned as she took a sip from her tea. "Something is troubling her. I thought she was happy here, but something in her past has hurt her badly, and she's afraid to care."

Daniel stared at her. "But what?"

"I don't know. Ever since Visiting Day, she's seemed quiet. I don't know what happened that day, but she was upset by something."

He thought of his time with her. Had he

upset her? He hoped not. She would be leaving, and he couldn't be emotionally involved with her. He needed to distance himself from her. To concentrate on work and looking into the property he'd viewed. That he and Emma had viewed. Daniel stood. "I need to get to work. I called in, but Fred wasn't too happy with me. I don't want to lose this job." He paused. "I don't think I can take Emma to work in the morning." *Or any other morning.* Not if he wanted to spend less time with her so that when it was time to go, it wouldn't hurt so much.

"Not to worry. I'll take her," Arlin said.

Daniel picked up his hat and headed toward the door. Leah and Henry followed him outside. They needed to open the store. Concern for Emma had brought them here. Emma. Not Jess. *Emma.* It bothered him that she hadn't trusted him enough to tell the truth. *She's an Englisher. She'd never be happy here.*

And that knowledge hurt.

She heard the sound of buggy wheels through her open bedroom window. Emma got up from the bed and went to peer outside. She didn't have a view of the yard. She could see the street, though, and she watched as one buggy left the property and turned left toward

Yoder's store while the other one pulled to the road and stopped. She didn't know why, but she knew it was Daniel. He waited until a car passed, then turned in the opposite direction of the store.

Daniel was upset with her, and she didn't blame him. Would he ever forgive her? The loss of his friendship would hit her hard. If things had been different, she would have liked to be more than Daniel's friend, but she knew that it wasn't meant to be. Her life was destined to be in the English world, a far cry from his life within the Amish community.

She drew away from the window and sat on the bed. Tears stung her eyes, but she refused to give in to them. She bent over and cradled her head in her hands. A knock on her bedroom door had her sitting up straight.

"Emma?" It was Missy.

She got up and opened the door. "Missy."

"I'd like to talk with you."

Emma nodded. "*Ja*, I figured you would." She sat down on the edge of the bed.

Missy entered the room and sat next to her. "What made you decide to leave now? Your birthday will be here before you know it, *ja*?"

She nodded. "I... I don't deserve to be here," she whispered. "You have all been so nice to me, and… there are things you don't know about me."

"That your real name is Emma Beiler?"

Emma gaped at her with shock. "How did you find out?"

"Daniel told me. He went looking for you this morning," Missy said. "He met a police officer who was displaying a photo of you in a coffee shop. He asked the officer questions but didn't let on that he knew you. He was surprised when the man told him your name was Emma and not Jess."

She closed her eyes. "I'm sorry. When I first met Leah, I didn't know who to trust. I thought it best if I gave a different name. Jess Morgan was a friend from school."

Missy studied her thoughtfully. "Emma, what made you leave now?"

"I felt bad. I was deceiving all of you, and I felt terrible…"

"I don't hold that against you. Arlin doesn't hold it against you. Leah and Henry would like you to come back to work at the store if you want. They trust you."

Emma blinked back tears. "Why?"

"Because they know your character. Do you think many people would *add* money to the register to repay someone for their kindness? You did. And Leah has always had *gut* instincts. I do, too. You need to stay here, Emma. If you leave again, you may be picked up by the police and sent back to your foster family. If you wait till your birthday, they can't make you go back."

"I know." Emma gazed at her with sorrow. "I'm sorry, Missy. I never meant to hurt you and Arlin. Or anyone." She thought of Daniel and knew that she'd hurt him most of all.

"You may work this afternoon if you'd like, but you don't have to. If you want to go back tomorrow, Arlin will take you. But the choice is yours."

"Arlin?"

Missy inclined her head. "Daniel has to work. He missed—"

"Work because of me." Emma averted her glance. "He is upset with me, and I don't blame him." She met the older woman's gaze. "Why are you being so nice to me?" She felt terrible. She still had secrets, which she couldn't confess, for she feared the consequences if she did.

"I was upset that you left, but you came back on your own," Missy said. She smiled. "You didn't want to leave, did you?"

"Nay, I like it here."

"Gut." Missy stood. "Because we like having you here. Why don't you come down for lunch? You can decide while you eat if you

want to work this afternoon or head in tomorrow morning."

"Missy," Emma began, "Arlin called me *dochter*."

The woman smiled. "Daughter. *Ja*, he considers you one of his."

Warmth filled Emma, and her heart overflowed with joy. "I haven't felt like a daughter in a long time," she whispered.

Missy eyed her with compassion and understanding. "Come. Arlin will be hungry."

Emma rose and followed the woman downstairs. Arlin was at the kitchen table. He looked over at her as she entered the room. "Arlin—"

"Sit, *dochter*. I'm hungry, aren't you?"

And just like that, Emma was forgiven. If she continued to feel guilty for having been banned from her own Amish community, she decided to make the best of it, for she knew she'd never again feel as included as she did right here in Arlin and Missy's home.

Would Daniel ever forgive her? she wondered. Or would she leave here with the knowledge that she'd lost the friendship and respect of the one man she longed to have in her life?

Chapter Fourteen

Emma climbed out of the family buggy after
Arlin and Missy. Today they were spending
Visiting Day with Meg and Peter Zook, Missy
and Arlin's daughter and son-in-law. When
the three of them approached the house, the
door opened, and a familiar young dark-haired
Amish woman with pretty features that clearly
resembled Missy's stepped out.

"Mam!" Meg greeted with a smile. She held
a young boy on her hip.

Missy smiled. *"Dochter."* She held out her
hands. "Is that my Timothy? It can't be! This
young man looks like he's three years old."

The boy reached for his grandmother with a
big toothy smile. *"Grossmamma.* I am three,"
he said, holding up three fingers as Missy
pulled him into her arms.

"Such a big boy," Emma said.

Timothy looked at her. "You are Emma, *ja*?"

She nodded. "That's right."

"You like cake? *Grossmamma* makes *gut* cake."

"*Ja*, I know. She's been teaching me how to cook and bake."

His face brightened. "Then you will be able to make cakes, too?"

"*Ja*." Emma caught Meg's gaze and smiled. The young woman looked amused, then love filled her eyes as she studied her son.

"Come in," Meg invited. "There is no reason for us to talk in the doorway.

A man came from the back of the house. "*Hallo*, Missy, Arlin. And 'tis Emma, *ja*?"

Emma nodded.

"Emma, do you remember my husband, Peter?"

"*Hallo*, Peter," she greeted with a smile. He was an extremely handsome dark-haired man who clearly loved his wife and young son.

Emma realized they were the first of the guests to arrive when she entered the kitchen and Meg invited Missy and her to sit at the kitchen table. Would any of the Lapps be coming? she wondered. She longed for a glimpse of Daniel. Arlin had taken her to and from work all week. She hadn't seen Daniel since he'd brought her home on Monday.

"Iced tea or soda?" Meg asked.

"Iced tea," Emma said. She rose. "May I help?"

"Nay, 'tis not necessary."

Arlin entered the room with Peter moments later. "Ah, iced tea. That looks *gut*."

Peter grinned as he went to a cabinet and pulled out two glasses. "We'll both have some," he said, and proceeded to pour his father-in-law and himself each a glass.

The five of them along with little Timothy, who climbed into his grandfather's lap, leisurely enjoyed their drinks until a knock on the front door heralded the arrival of Meg's sisters and their husbands—Charlie and Nate, Nell and James, and Leah and Henry.

Charlie grinned when she saw her. "You're looking much better than the first time we met."

Emma flashed the other couple an uneasy look. "*Danki*. I'm fine." She managed a smile for Nate, who placed a hand on Charlotte's shoulder.

Capturing Emma's gaze, Leah pulled her aside and smiled at her with warmth. Despite Emma's concern over how things would be between them after she'd left, Leah had been gracious and forgiving—almost like her departure and return had never happened.

"I'm so glad you came back to work with us." She smiled. "Henry is forever making me rest."

Henry chuckled as he joined them. "*Make* you?" He gazed fondly at his wife. "I don't *make* her do anything. Every afternoon, when she's dead tired on her feet, I simply steer her up to the house so that she can fall asleep at home rather than in a chair at the store counter."

"I appreciate that you allowed me back to work in the store."

"Nay," Henry said with a suddenly serious expression that made Emma's heart lurch with concern. "We appreciate you. We don't know what we would do without you."

"Henry..."

"He means it, Emma," Leah said softly.

Emma felt her throat tighten. *"Danki."* They both had been quick to forgive her. Would Daniel ever? She had not seen him in almost a week. Was he avoiding her? Hoping he wouldn't have to see her again before she left?

Henry nodded. "See? Emma understands."

The kitchen door opened and Katie and Samuel Lapp entered with Daniel, Joseph and Hannah close behind. Emma met Daniel's gaze, and her stomach filled with butterflies. He didn't smile at her. He greeted everyone but her, and she experienced a sadness that she knew she'd never get over. Daniel's parents greeted her, then were commandeered by Missy, who offered drinks and a light snack to start off the day. Much to her disappointment, Daniel and Joseph moved into the other room, leaving her with only their sister Hannah.

"Hannah, 'tis nice to see you," Emma said.

She tilted her head curiously. "So you ran away then came back, did you?"

Emma couldn't deny it. *"Ja."*

"Why?"

"I left because I thought I should. I came back because I realized I regretted leaving. I'm only here for a short time. Leaving the way I did hurt people I care about."

"Like Daniel," Hannah said.

She shrugged, then admitted, *"Ja,* like your *bruder."*

"He's upset, but I don't think he is really angry with you."

Hope filled Emma's heart. "He has every right to be."

"Maybe, but I'm glad you came back."

Emma blinked. "That's kind of you."

"Leah needs you. She's happy that you're here, so I am, too."

Joseph entered the room. "Emma. Daniel

said that Arlin has been taking you back and forth to work."

"*Ja*, he's been generous with his time."

"I didn't mind taking you home."

She gave him a genuine smile.

"I enjoyed our rides together," he admitted.

The look in his eyes startled her. "Joseph, I'll be leaving in less than two weeks."

Daniel's younger brother appeared surprised. "I didn't know." He seemed regretful but not upset. "Doesn't mean I can't give you rides until then, *ja*?" he said with a little grin.

Emma chuckled. "I suppose. I can talk with Arlin."

"Talk with Arlin about what?" Daniel said from behind her. She'd felt his presence immediately. He was the only man she'd ever felt a connection to. And he'd avoided her since the morning he'd found her walking back along the road.

Emma tensed. Then slowly turned toward him. He wore a green shirt that brought out the green flecks in his brown eyes. "Daniel," she acknowledged him.

"What about Arlin?" he asked, addressing Joseph without meeting her gaze once.

She felt the insult from head to toe. Was this what it was like to be shunned? To be ignored this way? "Excuse me," she said, and started to leave.

To her shock, Daniel grabbed her arm. "Where are you going?"

She tensed. "You don't want me here, so I'm leaving."

"Joseph, will you excuse us? I need to speak with Emma. Alone." Daniel hadn't let go of her arm, but his grip was gentle. "Emma, walk outside with me?"

Emma shot him a glance. He looked calm, determined, but she couldn't read his thoughts. "Fine."

He took her through the front door and walked toward the side of the house where there were no windows. There was a stand of evergreen trees there, a windbreak of sorts, although it was next to the house and not a farm field. Daniel stopped her there and stood face-to-face with her.

He gazed at her a long time without a single word. Then finally he asked, "Why did you run, Emma?"

Feeling ashamed, she averted her glance. "Daniel—"

"Why, Emma? Tell me. Was it because of me?"

Horrified by his assumption, she studied him with widened eyes. "What? Nay, Daniel—"

"Then *why*?"

"You wouldn't understand."

He narrowed his eyes. "Try me."

She rubbed a hand over her face. "There are things you don't know."

"What things? That your real name is Emma Beiler?"

Emma nodded. "Missy told me that you knew. But that's not all of it, Daniel, and I'm afraid I can't tell you. I can't. Please don't ask me to."

"You're leaving soon. What does it matter now?"

It mattered to her. If he—or anyone—knew, they would kick her out of their community, shun her as her own family had done. "It matters."

The fact that she would be leaving soon was hard enough. She couldn't bear it if he learned the truth and rejected her.

She heard him sigh heavily. "What are we going to do with you?" he whispered.

"What do you mean?" she asked shakily.

"Take a walk with me," Daniel said. He started toward the back of the property. He was quiet as they walked.

She grew tense to the point of pain. "Are you mad that I didn't tell you?"

"I was upset at first," he admitted, "but then

I realized that you did so because you were afraid to trust anyone."

She closed her eyes. "You're not angry."

He seemed to hesitate. "Nay."

It had been the longest week for Daniel. Knowing that she was near yet choosing to ignore her made him feel worse, not better. She would only be here a little while longer. Why deny himself her company until she left? All week he'd prayed to the Lord for guidance. He asked what he could do to get over her. He prayed that he could convince her to stay.

But it was clear to him that Emma still had secrets. The fact that she wouldn't tell him let him know that they had no future together, because she didn't trust him enough.

She looked pretty in a purple dress with white cape and apron with a white *kapp*. He was conscious of the fact that at full height she stood only to under his chin. As they walked, he stifled the urge to hold her hand. They weren't sweethearts, and she would be horrified if he took the liberty.

They strolled until they reached the back end of the stockade fence that contained Peter's livestock. Peter had taken over his father's farm. Horseshoe Joe, a blacksmith, had moved into the *dawdi haus*, but he continued to run his farrier business with Daniel's brother Jacob, leaving Peter with control of the main house and farm property.

Daniel took her to a quiet place behind the barn and halted where it was safe from prying eyes. "Emma, I want you to listen to me."

"What is it?" she asked, her voice shaking.

He felt himself pulled into the depths of her beautiful brown eyes. "Your birthday is coming up soon, and I know that you'll want to leave…but Leah is due to have her babies, and I was thinking that it would be a big help to them if you stayed until she gives birth. I know you've been handling the store alone while Henry takes Leah to her doctor's appointments and while she rests in the afternoons. Consider staying a little longer. Once the babies are born, other arrangements can be made."

Daniel wanted her to stay indefinitely, but he knew that wouldn't happen.

She appeared to give it some thought. "I do want to help Leah," she finally said.

She gazed out over the fields. There was a peacefulness about her features. He liked seeing her this way. Daniel held his breath as he waited for her answer. It would give him more time with her. Leah wasn't due to give birth until a few weeks after Emma's birthday.

"*Oll recht.* You make a good point. I'll stay until Leah gives birth."

He exhaled in relief. Daniel smiled. "*Danki*, Emma." Her agreement meant the world to him, although he couldn't let her know.

"I guess we should get back to the *haus* before Joseph and Hannah come looking for us." He started to walk away, but her hand on his arm stopped him. She released him immediately.

"Daniel?" she said quietly.

"*Ja?*" He gazed at her raised eyebrows.

"I'm glad you're no longer angry with me."

"Me, too, Emma."

Daniel took her back to the house, where they spent a quiet afternoon. Emma blended in well with his family. But he knew that unless he could convince her that Happiness was where she belonged, she would leave, and he'd never see her again.

Emma sat in a barn stall while Jeremiah slept, curled on her lap. She closed her eyes and leaned back against the wall, trying to stop her brain from thinking. Daniel entered her mind again, and she prayed for a sense of peace for what she had to do and for what surely would come after she left. It was late Monday. Despite Joseph's offer, Arlin continued to take her back and forth to work. They had gotten home about a half hour ago. She'd come here for a few minutes contemplation, to think about her promise to stay until Leah gave birth. She refused to hurt everyone by leaving abruptly, so she would do what she could and leave Happiness on good terms.

Emma heard a sound in the barn, letting her know that someone had entered. She straightened away from the wall as Leah appeared above the half door. Emma was surprised to see her.

"Leah, what are you doing here? Is something wrong?"

She greeted Emma with a smile. "Nay, I'm fine." She opened the door and came in. Emma noted how radiant her friend looked in a purple dress that enhanced her blue eyes and fit her swollen belly. "I thought I might find you here." She started to lower her pregnant self onto the floor next to Emma.

"Don't. I can stand."

Leah laughed as she studied the sleeping little dog and got down anyway. "I may need a hand getting back up."

"Why aren't you home resting?"

"I wanted to see you. What with all my doctor's appointments, we've barely had time to talk."

The little dog opened his eyes and perked up at the sound of Leah's voice. He swung his head, saw Leah and sprang from Emma's lap to greet her. Jeremiah stared at Leah's belly and hesitated as if he'd realized there was no room for him on her lap. Leah laughed, a melodious sound that spoke of joy as the Amish woman patted her side in invitation.

Emma watched with a smile as Jeremiah cuddled against Leah's side, enjoying the fingers that rubbed through the fur on his neck.

Emma saw Leah grimace. "Are you in pain?"

Leah smiled. "I'm fine. Just Braxton-Hicks contractions. My doctor warned me about them."

"Are you sure?"

"Ja." She smiled and appeared to relax. She resumed stroking Jeremiah's head and neck. Suddenly the little dog stood, trembled and stared at Leah.

"It looks like he wants something." Emma checked his water bowl. "He has plenty of water." She frowned as she eyed the dog. "What's wrong, boy?"

Suddenly, Leah gasped and cupped her belly. She tried to stand, and Emma immediately reached to help her. Her friend gave her a trembling smile. "I think I may be in labor."

Emma swallowed hard. "Where's Henry?"

"Up at the house."

"Stay here," Emma urged. "I'll get him." She stopped. "Is it *oll recht* to leave you alone for a minute?"

Leah nodded. "I'm fine." But she looked a bit shaky and a lot scared.

"It's not too early, is it?"

"Not for twins."

Emma drew a sharp breath. "Do you need a chair? Do you want me to help you outside?"

"Nay, just get Henry."

She nodded and raced to the house, bursting in through the kitchen to a number of startled gazes. "Leah is having twins!" she gasped.

Missy glanced at her with a smile. "*Ja*, we know."

"Nay! Now! She's in labor! Where's Henry?" Emma looked around the room frantically.

Having heard the commotion, Henry came rushing into the kitchen from another room. "What's going on?"

"Henry, you have to come now! Leah is in the barn and *she's in labor*!"

Henry paled and ran from the house.

Emma turned to see Missy following Henry. She wondered what she should do. Boil water? Get blankets? She wasn't a member of the family. She didn't have the right to interfere. *But Leah is my friend.*

Daniel entered the house a moment later. He walked in casually, clearly unaware of what was happening. "Where is everyone?"

"In the barn," Emma said, overcome with a sudden dizziness.

Suddenly, Daniel was by her side. He placed his hand lightly on her shoulder and slipped his other arm about her waist. "Don't faint on me."

She shook her head. "I won't. I'm fine." She gave in to the sensation of having him near, then promptly pulled away. "But Leah isn't," she gasped. "She's in the barn and she's in labor. *Leah is about to give birth!* I need to check on her." She pulled from the circle of Daniel's arms and ran from the house and sprinted toward the barn. Suddenly scared, she paused midway to catch her breath and stared at the outbuilding. Leah was inside. She desperately wanted to help her friend.

To her shock, Daniel was suddenly beside her. He captured her hand and gave it a light squeeze. "Leah will be fine. She's strong."

Emma nodded as she met his gaze. "What do we do?" She bit her lip. "Why are you here?"

"I wanted to see you," he said. "We have a few things to discuss. Arlin has been taking you to work. I want to give you a ride in the morning again. Joseph wants to bring you home, but I want to take you home, too."

"But Daniel, your work…"

"'Tis fine." He nodded. "I'll not be working there for much longer."

Henry and Missy came out of the barn holding Leah up between them. "I'm fine, Henry," Leah insisted. "Don't baby me!"

"Leah," her mother said patiently, "you need to be inside the *haus*," her mother said.

"Nay, I need to be at home." Leah turned her gaze up to her husband's. "Please, Henry, I want our babies to be born at *our* home."

Henry eyed his wife with concern. "Leah—"

Leah clutched at his arm. "Please, husband."

He nodded his head. He didn't look happy about it, but Emma knew that he would do what he could to please his wife.

Emma approached as Henry carefully eased Leah into their family buggy. His movements were loving, tender, and Emma felt a lump rise to her throat. She shuddered out a sigh and was surprised when Daniel put his arm around her. "Wouldn't it be better if we called a driver?"

She felt Daniel stiffen. "'Tis fine. They don't live far," he said crisply.

She met his gaze. "It's just…the road bumps might…"

His gaze softened. "I understand."

Emma wondered what would happen now. She'd promised Daniel that she would stay until Leah gave birth. Did that mean he wanted her to go before her eighteenth birthday? Or would Henry want her to run the store during Leah's recovery? She hoped so. She didn't want to leave yet. She wasn't eighteen, and the danger of being reunited with the Turners still loomed. But as painful as it would be, she desperately wanted a little more time with Daniel.

Missy approached her. "I'm going to follow them to the *haus*," she said. "Do you want to come with me?"

Surprise flared inside her, surprise and joy that Missy had included her as family by asking her to go. She flashed Daniel a glance to see that his expression was unreadable. Did he matter? She wanted to be there for Leah whether she had his support or not. But he didn't argue against her going, so maybe he didn't mind.

Everyone had come out into the yard to see Henry and Leah off. Missy murmured something to her daughters, and soon Missy and Emma were in a separate buggy following Henry and Leah with other family members bringing up the rear. As Missy steered the horse away from the house, Emma glanced back at Daniel. His features were taut with concern. For Leah? Or for her?

They arrived at Yoder's Country Crafts and General Store. Henry steered the carriage close to the house behind the store, and Missy parked beside him. She and Emma jumped out of their vehicle and followed the couple into the house.

"I'm fine," Leah assured them. "I can't be in labor."

"Your water broke. You will be feeling those pains within the next twenty-four hours," Missy said.

Emma watched as Henry pulled a chair from the kitchen table before he gently helped his wife to sit. "What can I do?" she asked.

Leah smiled at her. "You can sit and keep me company."

Henry and Missy nodded their approval, and Emma sat. "I'm sorry I'm not much help."

Leah scowled at her. "How can you say that? You ran for Henry."

"I shouldn't have left you," Emma insisted.

"Nonsense! And if you did, then where would I be? Giving birth in a barn."

"It wouldn't be the first baby born in a barn," Henry said softly.

Emma understood immediately and nodded.

He was referring to the baby who was born in a manger when there was no room at the inn.

The back door opened behind them, and Leah's sisters spilled into the kitchen. They had left their husbands back at the house. The men had told their wives that they would follow soon. The women were there for Leah. The men would come to support Henry.

"I'm hungry," Leah complained.

"Nay, *dochter*," Missy said. "'Tis better if you wait until after the babies are born. Eat now and you'll get sick to your stomach."

Leah looked at her mother with horror. "And if they stay inside me for another week? I'll starve!"

Leah's sisters laughed. Emma cracked a smile, because if the situation was amusing to the Stoltzfus sisters, then it meant that Leah would be fine.

The women spent the afternoon with Leah. There were no additional signs of labor. Finally, Leah told everyone to go home. "Doesn't look like it will happen anytime soon. *Mam*, I'd appreciate it if you'd stop by to tell Mary Smith, our midwife, then she'll be ready when we need her."

Missy looked as if she would refuse to leave. "We'll go now, but I'll be back later."

Leah nodded. Her gaze softened as it settled on Emma. "*Danki*, Emma."

Emma jerked with surprise. "Why are you thanking me?"

"Because you were there for me."

She leaned toward Leah. "You've always been there for me, Leah. I'd do anything for you." She paused. "Do you understand?"

Leah smiled. "*Ja*, I understand. Now go home and get some rest." Her gaze turned to encompass every woman in the room. "All of you. I may need you later."

Emma shot Henry a worried glance before she followed the women outside. Henry seemed composed, but in that quick look she noticed a flicker of anxiety in his blue gaze. Her belly fluttered with nerves as she climbed into the buggy beside Missy.

"Henry is scared," Emma said.

"We won't stay gone long. He's going to need us." Missy pulled into the paved driveway of a small house. "I won't be but a minute."

"The midwife's?"

"*Ja*," the older woman said with a smile. She was back within seconds. "Mary has all the details. She'll stop by later in an hour or so to check on Leah. We'll head back as soon as we can."

Emma thought about Daniel and her longing

to stay in Happiness and be his wife. She wondered how it would feel to be in Leah's shoes with Daniel as her loving husband and she soon to give birth to his child. Would he be frightened or calm when she went into labor? Would he gaze at her lovingly after she gave birth, look forward to raising their baby together?

Chapter Fifteen

Less than two hours later, Emma waited with Leah's family in the Yoder house. Missy excused herself to check on Leah. The women were in the kitchen. There was excitement in the air, as Leah's sisters were excited for the birth of their sister's twin babies. Ellie and her husband Reuben with their son Ethan were the first to arrive. Nell and James arrived minutes later. The men immediately went outside to chat after exacting a promise from their wives to keep them up to date on the babies' progress.

Daniel with his parents and siblings arrived next. Emma caught sight of him and longed to go to him. He had a way of making her see things clearly, and right now she was confused and felt like a mess.

Meg came with Peter and their son Timothy.

The sisters greeted Meg and urged Reuben to join the men outside.

"Reuben is nervous about Leah's babies," Ellie murmured quietly. "His first wife, Susanna, died after giving birth to Ethan." She smiled and touched her belly. "He's going to have to get used to it. I'm with child."

Everyone beamed at her. Emma smiled. "Congratulations."

Missy had returned and eyed Ellie with joy. "You'll take care of yourself, and Reuben won't have anything to worry about." Her daughter agreed. "I think I should go check on Leah."

Missy came back immediately. "It will happen soon. The midwife should be here any minute."

Mary Smith, the midwife, arrived, and after a quick hello she headed upstairs to see Leah. The women decided to put food on the table to distract themselves, and because the men were probably hungry. Ellie went to get the husbands, and they filed in, eager to eat.

There were muffins and biscuits and fresh bread. Everyone dug in. They were worried about Leah but eager to put their minds elsewhere even for just a few moments. The men filled up their plates and retreated into the great room.

Emma sat with the women at the kitchen

table and reached for a chocolate chip muffin. The breakfast treat had become a favorite after Missy had made them during her first week with them.

The midwife appeared in the doorway. "She's in labor now."

Missy nodded and stood. "Emma," she said, "Come with me."

Wide-eyed and heart beating wildly, Emma followed Missy up the stairs. When she entered the room, she found Leah in bed, propped up on pillows.

Leah smiled at her mother and Emma when she caught sight of them. "'Tis starting now, *Mam*."

Her mother smiled back. "It will be fine, *dochter*. I can't say I'm not surprised they're coming a little early. Twins usually come before they are due. You've carried them long enough. They should be fine."

"*Ja*, and you kept your doctor's appointments, took prenatal vitamins and had plenty of rest in the afternoons," Emma pointed out. "You will soon have two beautiful, healthy babies."

Leah's gaze went soft. "That's what Mary said." She shifted on the bed pillows. "Who's here?"

"Everyone," Emma said with awe. "Your sisters and their families. Your cousins and aunt and uncle."

Emma went downstairs to leave mother, daughter and midwife alone. She immediately spied Daniel leaning against the wall near the base of the stairway. She locked gazes with him.

"How is she?" he asked.

"She's doing well. The midwife thinks it won't be long now." She looked away. "Are you hungry?"

"I already ate, Emma."

She blushed. "*Ja*, of course."

"You seem nervous."

"Nay, just a bit taken aback." The evidence of Leah and Henry's love for each other was about to make an appearance. Emma wanted that. A husband to love and his children to love and nurture. But she'd never have that, because what she wanted was here and she couldn't stay. She didn't deserve to stay.

Emma peeked into the great room. Young Ethan lay on the floor close to his father's chair. Peter Zook, Meg's husband, held little Timothy asleep in his lap. Everywhere she looked in the room, there was evidence of love and family. Something that Emma didn't have.

Daniel approached. "Did you get any sleep?" he asked, studying her with his liquid brown eyes.

"Not much," she admitted. "I napped for

fifteen minutes or so before we decided to come here."

"I thought as much." His tone was gentle, his expression warm and understanding.

She stiffened. "I look that bad?"

He frowned. "Nay. You look…beautiful."

She blinked. He was so confusing. Why was he being so nice? She'd run away and come back, and it seemed as if he'd forgiven her, but did he really?

Time passed slowly, and the twins hadn't arrived yet. It was now morning and close to 8:00 a.m. Emma decided that she would go open the store. Henry would want her to. Leah would be glad that she'd stepped in. And it was just for today. She had no idea what would happen tomorrow.

She sought out Henry, who stood near his father-in-law. He was understandably tense and on edge. "Henry," she murmured as she approached. "I thought I'd open the store. It's almost time." Henry blinked as if in a daze, as if he didn't understand what she'd said. "The store," she repeated. "I'm going to open Yoder's for you."

He blinked. "You don't mind?"

Emma shook her head. "Nay. There are more than enough women here to help with

Leah. She needs her mother and sisters with her." She wasn't a sister. She didn't belong. "Where's the key?"

Henry grabbed the key from a kitchen drawer and gave it to her. "You know where to find me if you need help with anything."

Emma left the house and walked to the store. No one noticed she'd left, but it didn't matter. The sun lit up the morning sky, displaying autumn in its full splendor. She unlocked the back door and started the daily routine of getting ready for customers before she unlocked the front door. She doubted that anyone would come in the next hour or so, but she was prepared in case they did.

She pulled out two loaves of bread—one of German rye and the other a loaf of sliced white bread—from the storage room in the back. She carried and stashed them with the other lunch supplies under the counter near the wall end. Then Emma put on water to heat on the single gas burner for tea. When the water was hot, she fixed a cup of tea and sipped it leisurely as she looked around the store, deciding what else she should do today.

Her mind wandered to everyone back at the house. Would someone come tell her when Leah had her babies?

She heard a sound as someone entered the

store through the back door. Had she forgotten to lock it?

Daniel appeared in the door opening, his gaze settling on her immediately. "I thought you might like some company."

"Leah hasn't had the twins yet?"

He shook his head.

While she more than cared for Daniel, she didn't trust his motives for being here. "Water still hot?" he asked. When she nodded, he went behind the counter and made himself a cup of tea.

She wanted to spend time with him but also wondered if it wasn't wise to put distance between them so it wouldn't be so hard when she left.

"Don't you have to work today?" she asked more sharply than she'd intended.

Chapter Sixteen

Daniel was shocked by her attitude. "Is something wrong?"

Emma averted her gaze. "Nay," she said quietly. She appeared ashamed of her outburst.

"I don't believe you. Something is bothering you that you feel you need to take it out on me."

"Maybe you're the problem."

He narrowed his eyes. "Excuse me?" He saw her blush. "What have I done?"

She shook her head. "Sorry. I guess I'm just worried about Leah." She eyed him over her cup as she took a sip from her tea. "I appreciate your checking up on me, Daniel, but as you can see, I'm fine."

"Emma."

"Go back to the house, Daniel. I'm fine

here alone. You belong with your family. You should be with them."

"And you don't belong?"

"You said it. I didn't."

"Emma—"

"You don't need to worry about me. I'll be leaving soon."

He studied her, noting the sudden change in her brown eyes. She gazed at him blankly, as if she had no feelings for him, and it hurt. Despite her behavior, he caught a glimpse of vulnerability in the quiver of her pink lips and in a quick blink of her eyes. He inhaled a breath and realized that he loved her. He loved her, and she wouldn't stay.

"Daniel," she said sharply. "You're staring."

It was his turn to be embarrassed.

"Go up to the house. I've got this."

He struggled with disappointment. He wanted to stay and keep her company, but she wanted him to leave. She didn't need him. She'd only needed a place to hide in plain sight until she turned eighteen. Didn't she understand that she'd still be vulnerable, even after she came of age? That she could stay, and he could love and protect her?

He left the way he'd come, through the back door, and headed to the house. Because she was right. He should be there waiting with his family. And she didn't feel a part of that.

He wanted her to feel included. He wanted her to be a part of his family and his life.

Emma felt dejected after Daniel left the store. She'd told him to go, but still she missed him. She didn't deserve to have Daniel in her life…or the family who loved him. She'd leave and look back on her time here as something special, a moment when she'd enjoyed what she might have had if her parents hadn't left their Amish community. Mostly, she'd never forget Daniel Lapp, and she'd always wonder what happened to the man who'd stolen her heart.

In an effort to keep busy, she worked to clean the store. She swept the floor although there was little dirt to warrant the use of a good corn broom. She removed items and dusted shelves before putting the merchandise back. Then she went to the counter again where she found paper and pen, then jotted down the items that needed to be reordered.

The front door jingled. Emma looked up from the paper with a smile on her face with the hope that Daniel had returned despite her efforts to push him away. She gasped in horror as a man approached. He didn't stop until he reached the counter. She'd recognize his smirk anywhere. The man was Bryce Turner, her foster father.

"What are you doing here?" she demanded. She attempted to keep calm as she casually searched for something to use as a weapon in case she needed to defend herself. "What do you want?"

"I've come to take you home, Emma dear." He stared at her, a big brute of a man with an unholy light in his black eyes.

"This is my home now. I have family and friends here."

Bryce laughed. "You're living with the Amish?" His gaze ran down the length of her as if noting her plain clothing and prayer *kapp* for the first time. "I don't think so. I'll have a talk with them. I'm sure they'll be happy to see you go."

"Bryce, please. Just leave. You don't need me. Keep the money from the state. I don't care. The authorities won't know that I'm no longer living with you. I'll be eighteen soon anyway and free to live on my own."

The man's expression hardened. "It sounds like you don't want to come home with me. After everything I've done for you, that's not very nice. You shouldn't talk that way to your foster father." He snarled, "Show some respect."

She flinched. He had edged to the end of

the counter, boxing her in. She wondered what would happen if she attempted to bolt out the back door. Emma recalled the pain he'd inflicted on her arm and the resulting bruises. Her arms were finally healing, and she refused to allow him to hurt her again.

She sighed, and her shoulders slumped. She didn't want to cause trouble for her Amish friends. She needed to keep the man as far from them as she could...even if she was forced to go with him. *Keep him talking until you can figure a way to escape him.*

"How did you find me?"

"I had some help. The police were looking for you when they found someone who thought they'd seen you. The tip didn't amount to anything concrete, so I came looking for you myself. I knew you had to be close. After all, you once lived in an Amish community when you were a child."

"How did you know that?"

"We received a file on you. Or should I say, I hired someone to investigate your background. We couldn't have a criminal living in our house."

Then his features darkened. "You saw us, didn't you?" he murmured.

"What?"

"Don't play innocent now. You saw me and

Kent in the alley that night. I figured you had because you ran away soon after." His mouth tightened into a thin line. "Let's go," he ordered.

"I'd rather stay here."

"I'm not asking. I'm telling you to get moving or suffer the consequences."

She stiffened her spine. No, she thought, she couldn't go back. She *wouldn't*.

With a suddenness that shocked her, Bryce grabbed her by the arm and dragged her from behind the counter. His fingers squeezed flesh, making her cry out with pain. "Move!" he commanded. "Did you honestly think I wouldn't come after you?" He pulled her the length of the store.

"What are you going to do with me?" she gasped.

"Why, dear Emma, I won't do anything. You're my daughter, and I take good care of my children."

"I'm not your child and I don't want to go!" she cried, struggling against his hold in an effort to get free.

"Sorry, sweetheart, but you're going. Get moving or I'll force you."

She fought harder, but Bryce only laughed as he dragged her out of the store and toward his car.

Emma saw a little English girl playing across the street and quickly looked away. Bryce must have sensed the direction of her gaze, because he hollered across the street to the child. "Hi, honey," he said. "My friend and I are going for a ride."

"No!" Emma screamed.

The girl jumped up and backed away.

Bryce cursed. "You tell anyone what you've seen, little girl, and I'll come back to get you," he warned.

The child crouched on the lawn to play with her dolls, as if he hadn't spoken. Bryce stared at the child a long moment, then, assured of the little girl's silence, he opened his car door and pushed Emma inside. "Get in! Now!" he ordered when she tried to resist him.

Emma was terrified. She'd never get to see Daniel again...or any of the others here she regarded as family. She could only imagine what would happen to her if she didn't find a way to escape. Bruising would be the least of her worries. There were other things that Bryce could do to ensure her silence.

Daniel was upset. He stood in the great room in the house, waiting for Leah to give birth while Emma was working alone in the store. He frowned. Why didn't she want him there?

They'd been friends, and he felt sure she had feelings for him. What made her behave that way? Why wouldn't she tell him what was bothering her?

Leah was in labor. The men were chatting like they were at a picnic outside. Except for Henry. Leah's husband looked ill with worry. No doubt, he wanted to be upstairs with his wife.

Emma. He wanted to see her. He needed to be with Emma, because he loved and needed her. Now if only he could convince her of that.

He decided to head back to the store to see her. He loved her. He would convince her to talk to him. If she cared for him even a little, he'd work to convince her that he was the right man for her. That the Amish community was the right home for her.

This time he entered through the front entrance. "Emma?" There was no sign of her.

Calling her name repeatedly, he checked in the back rooms but couldn't find her anywhere.

Would she leave without a word? Nay, she wouldn't! She'd promised to stay. And Leah had yet to give birth. Besides, Emma was still only seventeen. Those were two good reasons for her to stay.

She'd left the store unlocked. That wasn't like her. He grew more concerned. Where was she? If she had left of her own free will, she would have locked up the store and put the key where Henry could find it.

What if the police had found her? Or worse yet, her foster father?

Daniel burst out of the store toward the street. He looked both ways but saw no sign of her anywhere. A little girl played in the yard across the street. Had she seen Emma? He approached her.

"Hallo," he said gently. "Did you see a woman leave the store?" He smiled. "An Amish woman?"

Fear entered her green eyes as the child looked up at him. She nodded but didn't speak.

Encouraged, Daniel crouched beside her. "Was anyone with her?"

The girl nodded vigorously.

"Can you tell me what you saw?" He frowned when she shook her head. "But you saw something?"

She bobbed her head.

"Was she with a man?"

"Yes," she whispered.

"Please," he begged, "she may be in danger. I need to know what you saw."

The child looked thoughtful. "A bad man took her," she finally said.

"A bad man?" His stomach roiled with dread and fear.

"Yes, they came out of that store together, and he shoved her into his car." She clutched her doll tightly to her chest. "She didn't want to go. The lady didn't want to leave with him, but he made her."

"What color was the car?"

"Blue." She looked up at him with rounded eyes. "She didn't want to go," she repeated, clearly frightened. "She tried to get away, but he wouldn't let her. Then he saw me and said he'd come back to get me if I told." She trembled. "You won't let him get me, will you?"

"No one will hurt you," he soothed. "Where is your mother?"

"She's at work. My babysitter is inside."

"I'm going to get help from the police. Why don't you go inside where it is safe? When I bring a policeman, will you let us in? Tell your babysitter—what's her name?"

"Patty."

Daniel nodded "Tell Patty that we'll be coming to talk with you. Will you do that?"

"Yes."

"Get your dolls and take them safely inside with you."

He rose to his feet. "Thank you for telling what you saw. The lady—she's special to me."

"You're going to get her back?"

"Yes. I'll do everything I can to get her

back." He gave her a gentle smile. "Now go inside." Daniel watched as she ran to her house, then he sprinted across the street and up to the house. He burst in the room where the men waited. "Henry, do you have your cell phone? I need to use it."

"Ja." Henry frowned at him. "Something wrong?"

"Emma has been kidnapped."

Chapter Seventeen

Emma sat in the back of Bryce Turner's sedan, amazed that he hadn't tied her up, that he believed she wouldn't attempt to escape. But he was wrong. Yes, she was scared, even terrified, but the first chance she got, she'd escape and return to Happiness, to those she cared about.

She pressed her face against the rear passenger window. She studied her surroundings. They hadn't gone far, so they were still in Lancaster County. She heard the ding that accompanied the low-fuel light in Bryce's car. It was only a matter of time before he'd have to pull into a gas station and refuel. As the man drove down the road, Emma recognized the restaurant across the street. Thank the Lord that they were still on the main road.

She longed to go back. Home, she thought.

Happiness was the first place to feel like home since she'd left Indiana.

She heard Bryce curse and watched with satisfaction as he pulled the car into a gas station. Emma hid a smile as he got out to fill up the car with gas.

He leaned in and glared at her. "Stay where you are," he ordered. "Or there'll be consequences."

She waited with patience as Bryce pumped gas. When he was done, he growled with anger when he wasn't given a printed receipt at the pump. She sat back and closed her eyes and pretended to have fallen asleep. She waited a few moments until Bryce entered the building to get his receipt.

It's now or never! Emma threw open the door and bolted down the street back the way they'd come. When she heard Bryce's outraged yell, she raced across a farm field toward a large house set off from the road. She prayed for help as she ran, begged God to find her help.

She banged hard on the farmhouse door. When no one came to open it, she hammered her fist against the wood. *"Answer the door. Please!"* But no one came.

She looked back. Bryce was near the edge of the road, searching for her. She knew the exact moment he spotted her and headed her way. She changed direction, skirted the house and raced back to the road. She heard him bellow at her to stop, but she kept on going.

Daniel. Thoughts of him comforted her until Emma felt a strong, punishing grip on her arm. Bryce's furious face loomed above her. His fingers tightened painfully above her forearm. "Let me go!"

"Shut up! Stop or I'll punch you out so you can't yell for help!"

She slumped as if defeated. She wanted him to think that she was biddable, for if he decided to tie her up, she'd never ever be free of him.

Emma prayed as he dragged her toward his car. *Please, Lord, help me. I'll do better, I promise. I'll apologize. I'll do whatever You want. Please.*

"No sense praying, girl. He won't listen to the likes of you."

She ignored him and closed her eyes as she continued to pray. She ignored the pain of his hold and put her trust in the Lord.

Suddenly, she heard police sirens. Bryce seemed surprised, and Emma took the opportunity to be free of him again and run. Bryce chased after her, catching her before she got more than a few yards. Two police cars roared up to surround her and Bryce. She froze. Would he convince them that she was his misbehaving daughter? Would they insist she go home with him? She wouldn't be forced this time! She'd hold her ground and demand they listen to the truth about Bryce.

Officers encircled them with drawn guns. Bryce smiled. "I'm glad you came, officers. I've been searching everywhere for my daughter. I'm grateful I found her. Thanks to you, I have her back."

"Step away from the girl, Mr. Turner," an officer ordered.

"Why are you aiming your gun at me?" Bryce said with outrage. "I haven't done anything wrong. She's the one who ran away. I only came to bring her home."

"I don't know, Doug," one officer said to another. "The girl sure looks Amish to me. Doesn't look like she's this man's daughter."

"I'm not," Emma said, then cried when Bryce dug his fingers into her arm. The pain made her waver dizzily.

"Release her and put up your hands, Turner," a third officer said.

When Bryce didn't move, he stepped closer, gun aimed directly at Bryce.

Bryce released her and held up his hands. "You're making a mistake," he warned.

Out of breath, Emma leaned over and gulped

for air. Tears ran down her face, and she couldn't stop them.

Someone knelt at her side, gently touching her shoulder. "Emma," said a familiar voice.

She turned her head. "Daniel," she breathed.

"*Ja*, dear heart." He was careful as he helped her to straighten. He put his arm around her, and Emma felt safe and protected...and loved. Overwhelmed with emotion, she sobbed, and Daniel pulled her into his arms.

"Emma, 'tis *oll recht*. I'm here now. I won't let anyone hurt you again."

Daniel held her close as she answered the police officers' questions truthfully about her life with the family, about what crimes she'd witnessed involving the man and his son. Once she'd finished answering questions, the officers took Bryce into custody and loaded him, handcuffed, into the back of a police cruiser.

Daniel was silent as he drove her back to Leah and Henry's. She wondered what he was thinking.

"You came for me," she whispered. "Why?"

Daniel shot her a concerned look. "You were gone. The store was open, and I knew you wouldn't leave it unlocked. Then I saw the little girl across the street. She told me what she'd seen. So I called the police and then I followed them." She felt his shudder. "Fortunately, you hadn't been taken far."

Emma sighed. "Thank you. I was shocked to see Bryce." She shuddered and hugged herself. "I… I don't think I would have gotten away from him alive."

"You never told the police what you saw until today."

"Because the police never believed me. When I ran away the first time, I tried to tell them how bad things were for me at the Turners', but they wouldn't listen. Bryce convinced them I was a troubled teen who needed love." She paused as she fought tears. "I was just a runaway foster kid, and Bryce was a law-abiding citizen. The physical abuse wasn't obvious back then…"

Daniel remained silent as he steered the horse into the driveway and up the hill toward Leah and Henry's house. As she followed Daniel into Leah and Henry's house, Emma saw pleased smiles on everyone in the great room. Charlie rushed over and reached for her hand. "Are you *oll recht*?"

Emma smiled, sensing her genuine concern. "I'm fine."

Henry approached, his features filled with happiness. "Leah delivered our babies. We have twin sons! I'm a *dat*!"

Emma beamed at him. "Congratulations."

Daniel rested a gentle hand against her lower back and asked Henry, "When can we see them?"

"As soon as Arlin and Missy come downstairs. I thought it best to not overwhelm them with too many at one time."

"How is Leah?" Emma asked. Leah had been a true friend to her. She wished the woman every happiness that life had to offer.

"She's well," Henry said with a bright smile. "Happy."

Everyone had to wait their turn. Her sisters and their husbands were allowed to go in together before the others. When it had come time for the actual birthing, the midwife had asked everyone to leave except Missy, the babies' grandmother. She'd stayed until Arlin came into the room with Arlin's sister Katie and her husband Samuel. After they had enjoyed the sight of Arlin's new grandsons, they had rejoined the others downstairs. Finally, Leah's cousins were allowed in. Emma was prepared to hang back until everyone had enjoyed their turn. Hannah, Joseph and Daniel were called up to take a peek.

Daniel turned toward Emma. "Come with us," he urged softly.

She blinked with surprise. She looked at

Henry, who nodded and smiled his approval. Overjoyed to be included, Emma accompanied him up the stairs to the second floor.

The sight that met Emma nearly stole her breath. Her friend was propped up by pillows with a tiny newborn in each arm. Her gaze met Emma's as the four of them entered the room. Her eyes suddenly lit up as Henry came in behind them. He went immediately to Leah's side and stared at her adoringly. Emma was overwhelmed with emotion when Henry reached out to stroke a gentle finger over each of his tiny sons' foreheads.

Leah waved the four newcomers closer. "Come and meet our sons, Isaac Henry and Daniel James."

Emma felt Daniel tense, and she smiled when Leah explained, "Isaac for Henry's closest friend with his middle name after Henry. Our other son is named after you, Daniel. You have always been there for us when we needed you. And James? It seems fitting that we give him the name of a man who gave up his English life because he loves my sister."

Daniel seemed overcome with emotion. Emma wanted to reach for his hand but didn't dare. He had offered her comfort when she needed it, but this was different. This wasn't pain or sadness. This was joy.

The cousins were enjoying their visit with the newborns. Daniel pressed her forward to get a closer view of the tiny little boys in Leah's arms.

As she studied their little features, then turned to observe their parents, who were in love and overjoyed with their family, she felt a longing so deep she was on the verge of tears.

She stepped back, and Daniel came to stand by her side. She loved the man next to her, but unfortunately her time here in Happiness with everyone, with Daniel, was coming to an end.

"I want that," Daniel whispered in her ear as he leaned close, "with you."

She gaped at him. "What?"

His smile was warm with affection…and love. She shook her head, for she couldn't believe what she'd heard. Had he just admitted that he cared for her? Maybe even loved her?

"Daniel—"

With his mouth close to her ear, he whispered, "I want a life with you, Emma. I want to marry you and have a family with you."

She wanted this so badly, she couldn't believe it was happening. "Daniel, there is something you don't know, and it might change how you feel about me."

Daniel frowned. "I don't believe that, Emma. You won my heart with your determination to do the right thing." He reached for her hand, murmured that they were going downstairs so others could see the babies. "Leah. Henry. *Danki*. I'm honored that you chose to name your son after me."

Then he pulled Emma from the room. Daniel tugged her through the house and then outside.

Emma halted him as soon as they stepped out. "I can't stay. I…"

"What, Emma?" he asked gently.

She felt her face crumple as she started to cry. "You won't want me here, Daniel. Promise me that I can say *gut* bye to everyone before I go."

He frowned. "Tell me."

"I've been shunned."

Daniel studied the distraught woman before him and wondered what she was talking about. Emma was regretful. That alone made him wonder why she thought she'd been shunned.

"I used to live in an Amish community in Indiana. When I was younger, my parents left the church and took me with them. They told me that we could never go back to visit my *grosseldre* or any of our relatives, because we'd been shunned."

"Emma, you were how old?"

"Six," she breathed.

He smiled at her warmly. He saw her confusion and went on to quickly explain. "You were six years old, Emma. You were not a member of the church. You were never shunned. Your parents were, because they joined the church and decided to leave anyway. That is an offense against the Ordnung. Going with your parents because you were six and had to remain with your parents is not, Emma. You are not shunned."

She reeled as if in shock. "But they told me—"

"They couldn't go back, but you could have."

Her eyes filled with tears. "After they died, I could have gone back to live with my family in Indiana?"

"*Ja.*"

Emma began to weep.

"I hate that you went through this, believing as you did. That you had to endure the Turners and what they did to you. But if you had gone to live with your *grosseldre*, then I never would have met you."

She blinked. "*Ja*, you're right," she breathed with awe.

"Do you want to go home to Indiana, Emma? Or would you consider staying here in Happiness with me? I love you, Emma Beiler. I want you here with me. When you're ready, I want you to be my wife." He smiled at her. "Earlier today I put an offer in for that property. The owner accepted it, and I put down a deposit. That's why I didn't pick you up this morning. I had to work this afternoon, but I came to see you as soon as I got off work." He took hold of her hands. "I won't be working for Rhoades Construction for much longer. In fact, I put in my two weeks' notice. I'll be opening my harness shop. I thought that once we marry, we'll live in the house we looked at. What do you think?"

Her eyes shone with happiness. "I'd like that very much."

"Gut."

"Daniel?" she murmured softly.

"Ja?"

"I'd like to see my family in Indiana."

"Ja, you should," he said approvingly. "And we can invite them to our wedding."

"Danki, Daniel."

"And you no longer have to worry about the Turners. I have a feeling Bryce and his son will be put in jail for their drug dealing and the abuse you suffered at their hands."

Emma beamed at him. "I love you, Daniel."

"I love you, Emma."

Epilogue

A year later, Emma and Daniel wed before the Amish community in Happiness. Only weeks before, Daniel and Emma had joined the Amish church. Daniel with Emma's help had set up his harness shop on the property he'd purchased. He'd accepted his father's help with financing because he wanted to own his home before he married Emma.

Emma stood beside Daniel as they made their vows. She was overwhelmed with love for her new husband. He had proved time and again over the last months how much he loved her. He found her first foster parents whom she'd loved. John Bowden's cancer was in remission, and he and May were happy to attend the wedding.

Emma's family from Indiana were seated among the congregation. They had been stunned to hear what happened to her and were happy to be a part of her life again. Their pleasure was twofold when they saw that Emma had found love and a new life in an Amish community.

After the wedding reception was over, Daniel and Emma, alone in their new home, gazed at each other in the waning light of a beautiful autumn day.

Emma smiled at her husband. "I love you. More than you'll ever know."

"Wife, I'll love you forever." Daniel pulled her into his arms and kissed her.

As she leaned into him, Emma sent up a silent prayer of thanks. She had everything she'd ever wanted—Daniel, a family and the promise of a future blessed by God.

* * * * *

*If you loved this story,
check out the other books
in Rebecca Kertz's miniseries
Women of Lancaster County.*

A Secret Amish Love
Her Amish Christmas Sweetheart
Her Forgiving Amish Heart
Her Amish Christmas Gift
His Suitable Amish Wife

Available now from Love Inspired!

*Find more great reads at www.LoveIn-
spired.com*

Dear Reader,

If this isn't your first visit to Happiness in Lancaster County then you've most likely met the Lapp family—Samuel and Katie Lapp with their eight children, especially their five oldest sons who each found love in my Lancaster County Wedding books. In the Women of Lancaster County series, you meet the five Stoltzfus sisters, who happen to be the Lapp siblings' cousins, who also find true love.

In *Finding Her Amish Love*, Emma Beiler is a runaway foster child who returns to Happiness after escaping her Maryland foster home for the second time. Emma doesn't want anyone to learn that she was raised in an Amish community until the age of six, when her family left for an English life. When she is given a temporary home and job in Leah's community, Emma worries that if anyone learned the truth about her past, she'd be sent away. She needs a safe place to stay until she's eighteen, when she'll be free of the foster care system.

Daniel Lapp discovers Emma sleeping in the barn on his cousin Ellie's property. He helps Emma and eventually develops feelings for her. He doesn't know that Emma has lied about her identity.

I hope you enjoy Emma and Daniel's story during which Emma finds a place within the Stoltzfus family and a forever home with the man she loves.

I wish you joy, good health and many blessings.

Love and light,
Rebecca Kertz

INTRODUCING OUR
FABULOUS NEW COVER LOOK!
COMING FEBRUARY 2020

Find your favorite series in-store, online or subscribe to the Reader Service!

Get 4 FREE REWARDS!

We'll send you 2 FREE Books
plus 2 FREE Mystery Gifts.

Love Inspired® Suspense books feature Christian characters facing challenges to their faith... and lives.

THE FORTUNES OF TEXAS COLLECTION!

18 FREE BOOKS in all!

Treat yourself to the rich legacy of the Fortune and Mendoza clans in this remarkable 50-book collection. This collection is packed with cowboys, tycoons and Texas-sized romances!

YES! Please send me **The Fortunes of Texas Collection** in Larger Print. This collection begins with 3 FREE books and 2 FREE gifts in the first shipment. Along with my 3 free books, I'll also get the next 4 books from The Fortunes of Texas Collection, in LARGER PRINT, which I may either return and owe nothing, or keep for the low price of $5.24 U.S./$5.89 CDN each plus $2.99 for shipping and handling per shipment*. If I decide to continue, about once a month for 8 months I will get 6 or 7 more books but will only need to pay for 4. That means 2 or 3 books in every shipment will be FREE! If I decide to keep the entire collection, I'll have paid for only 32 books because 18 books are FREE! I understand that accepting the 3 free books and gifts places me under no obligation to buy anything. I can always return a shipment and cancel at any time. My free books and gifts are mine to keep no matter what I decide.

☐ 269 HCN 4622   ☐ 469 HCN 4622

Name (please print)

Address   Apt. #

City   State/Province   Zip/Postal Code

Mail to the Reader Service:
IN U.S.A.: P.O. Box 1341, Buffalo, N.Y. 14240-8531
IN CANADA: P.O. Box 603, Fort Erie, Ontario L2A 5X3

AN UNLIKELY AMISH MATCH
Indiana Amish Brides • by Vannetta Chapman

Susannah Beiler is determined to keep her friends from falling for the new bad-boy Amish bachelor in town—even if it means keeping an eye on Micah Fisher herself. But when she gets to know him, can she protect her own heart?

THE AMISH WIDOW'S HEART
Brides of Lost Creek • by Marta Perry

After her husband's death, Bethany Esch must help his business partner run the local Amish general store. But as she starts to care for Daniel Miller, she'll have to make a choice: let her husband's recently discovered secrets come between them...or learn to trust again.

THE WRANGLER'S LAST CHANCE
Red Dog Ranch • by Jessica Keller

When Carter Kelly is hired as the head wrangler at Red Dog Ranch, the self-proclaimed wanderer doesn't plan to stay long. But as he helps Shannon Jarrett plan a horse show fund-raiser and gain self-confidence after her abusive past relationship, will he finally find a home...and love?

THEIR WANDER CANYON WISH
Wander Canyon • by Allie Pleiter

Back in her hometown with her twin daughters, widow Marilyn Sofitel is set on never falling in love again. But after spending time with town rebel Wyatt Walker as he works to fix the carousel her girls love, she can't help but wish he could be a part of their fresh start.

HER ROCKY MOUNTAIN HOPE
Rocky Mountain Heroes • by Mindy Obenhaus

Ready to open his camp for young cancer patients, Daniel Stephens must impress foundation overseer Blythe McDonald to ensure she approves funding for next year. But can he convince the cautious former cancer patient his camp is worthy of the money...and that he's worthy of her heart?

A MOTHER'S SECRET
by Gabrielle Meyer

Single mother Joy Gordon must find a way to keep her home after the death of her elderly benefactor, who allowed her family to stay there. But she never expects to see Chase Asher—the secret father of her twin girls—there to sell the house.

LICNM0120